Sins of the Syndicate

LEXXI JAMES

With Grateful Appreciation to My Remarkable Editing Team

Cate Hogan, Pam Berehulke, & Jaime Ryter

With Special Thanks to Rebecca Mysoor

Cover by Book Sprite, LLC

Image by Wander Aguiar

Wander Aguiar Photography LLC

Model Sam Myerson @sammyerson

This is a work of fiction. Names, characters, places, and incidents are the product of the author's imagination. Specific named locations, public names, and other specified elements are used for impact, but this novel's story and characters are 100 percent fictitious. Certain long-standing institutions, agencies, and public offices are mentioned, but the characters involved are wholly imaginary. Resemblance to individuals, living or dead, or to events which have occurred is purely coincidental. And if your life happens to bear a strong resemblance to my imaginings, then well done and cheers to you! You're a freaking rock star!

CHAPTER 1

Ivy

"I'm here to see Ms. Palmer."

The man's voice is deep, with an authority that makes me wonder why he requested his tour of the assisted living center with me. His suit is expensive but not overly fitted. And the dark gray is a stark contrast to the clear blue of his eyes. The silvery accents in his well-trimmed salt-and-pepper hair give him the air of distinction, with professional charm brimming from behind what seems to be a practiced smile.

It's not unlike the smiles I'm used to from people clinging to their courtesy as they navigate a world of decisions. How will I care for my loved one? Will they be safe? Is this covered by insurance? How much will it cost?

If money is no object, the ones with the deepest pockets land here. Except for me. It took two years for me to work off my mom's debt, and it gave me a lifetime's worth of watching people in return. I remind myself that I'm here to ease them into a relationship of trust and support. Not to pressure them with a hard sell, despite those very words from my boss.

"I'm Ivy," I say, stepping out from behind the long reception desk. I hold out a hand, meeting his solemn smile with one of my own as he takes my hand for a brief shake. "And you're Mr.—"

"Sin," he says, scanning the lobby and halls. I can't tell if he's overwhelmed or underwhelmed, but he avoids meeting my eyes as he glances around. "Call me Sin."

"All right, *Sin*."

I've already seen the roster, noting that the tour request was made by a Bryce Jacob Sinclair, Esquire. The formal name suits him as equally as the nickname Sin. A gravity and authority harden the lines of his face, hiding whatever's lurking just below the surface.

The heaviness that drags him down threatens to pull me with it, an occupational hazard to a career dependent on emotional connection and empathy. When his expectant eyes meet mine, I snap back to work.

Handing him a visitor badge, I gesture down the north hall. "This way."

Along our tour, Sin asks the usual questions: How many occupants are there? What's the caregiver-to-resident ratio? If the staff live on the premises—which feels more like he's asking if *I* live on the premises.

No matter how many times I give this tour, I'm delighted when he asks about the one thing that always connects us, though it never seems to at first. Mr. Whiskers.

The small fluffy toy is weightless in my hand as I tug it from the pocket it's been peeking out from and hold it up.

I'm not the only one beaming at the sight of him. Even the stone-faced Sin cracks a smile, albeit a very small one. It creases his face enough that I peg him to be about sixty, which makes me wonder if he's looking at the facility for his mother or possibly his wife.

"This is Mr. Whiskers."

"Your stuffed animal?" Sin's studious eyes move from it to me, the intensity of his gaze so much harsher than is warranted by my crazy talk.

Unnerved, I take in a breath. "Mr. Whiskers is so much more than that. He's a therapy stuffed animal. You can even pop him in the microwave to warm him up."

I avoid talking about my past or that Mr. Whiskers has been my personal security blanket for nearly twenty years.

Sin nods. "Do all residents get a toy? Or just the bad ones?" His contempt doesn't bother me. He doesn't understand, and it's my job to help him understand.

"Sparrow Wellness and Assisted Living is unlike any facility you may have seen. Our occupants range in age from twenty to eighty-two. Sometimes, a little non-threatening toy is a great way for people to open up. I didn't have to say a word about him, and you asked."

His face is stone. No hint as to whether he's annoyed or amused. His eyes wander through the opening to a vacant room. "Continue."

"Even if they aren't interested in a little support from a cuddly friend, he's a big hit with the children who visit. We keep a small stockpile in the back."

"Trauma victims?" He mutters the question under his breath in a way that sounds less like distaste and more like hope.

"We cater to a wide range of conditions, trauma being just one of them. Some residents have degenerative conditions that require more care than their families can provide. Others don't have families, in which case we become their family if their physician recommends us."

Sin takes several steps into the room, moving his gaze from the warm cream walls and big bay window to me. "Looking for a family, Ms. Palmer?"

His tone is sharp and icy, with enough condescension that I have to remind myself that people in pain tend to inflict pain. He's just hurting, and I'm the closest target within striking distance. But it's not directed at me. *Even if it is the truth.*

"Just looking to help as many people as I can." I hold my smile as I step away, shooing off a flurry of emotions that I'll need to deal with later. For now, Sin is in his role of distrustful client. It's up to me to win him over.

His brisk footsteps close in quickly from behind.

We stop at the courtyard, where a few residents have opted to spend their morning lounging on lawn furniture, enjoying the sun. We walk in silence. He takes an interest in a resident, Angie, lost in the strokes of a painting she's creating. I use the time to take a closer look at his paperwork, only now noticing he's left several areas blank.

It's not uncommon. People tend to be guarded their first time walking through. It's a long way from *nice to meet you* to *I trust you with my loved one*, but it's a familiar road I've traveled many, many times.

"It's you," Sin says, and I look up.

Seeing the painting this close, I realize the resemblance is uncanny. I'd almost believe it was me if not for the elegance of the off-the-shoulder gown Angie has painted her in, or the delight in her eyes that could never radiate from mine. It's how I want to look. Confident. Complete. Happy. Instead, my heart is riddled with so many holes, half the time it feels like it's about to collapse under all the damage.

Taking a closer look, I see the white curl in her subject's curly black hair—identical to the one that inexplicably grows at my right temple. Angie nods, beaming with a grin as she silently lets me know it is me.

It's a version of me that could only happen in Angie's beautiful imagination.

Grateful, I hug Angie, being gentle to avoid overdoing it. Her muscles are weak. Every word from her lips is a fight, but they're always worth waiting for. Especially today as she sounds out two words.

"H-h-hap-p-py b-b-b-irth-d-day."

My heart leaps as she completes the short sentence. It's the most she's said in a week, and I find myself speechless, if not a bit teary-eyed.

"Sorry, do you mind if I steal Ivy for a second?"

Derrick interrupts, probably to keep me from outright blubbering. He's more than my boss, though no one would know it. We've been a couple for nearly a year but keeping our relationship under wraps was his idea as much as mine. Sort of.

I keep one eye on Sin, watching as he carries on a one-sided conversation with Angie. He doesn't seem concerned that she isn't responding. On the contrary, his smile is genuine, even though he receives nothing more than a few polite nods back. But I'm ready to jump in if he demands any more.

Derrick's hands stay pocketed, the way they always do when he's hiding something. Maybe it's a surprise. Like dinner at a fancy restaurant on the waterfront. Or cuddling together in front of a romantic bonfire on the beach.

Between his work schedule and mine—which is a result of his —it's been weeks since I've had any action. I'm bursting at the seams with sexual frustration, so if my birthday celebration is a beer, a grilled cheese, and twenty solid minutes of hitting it hard during whatever sci-fi show he can't live without, I'll take it.

I'm grinning like an idiot when he says low, "I really need you to bring this one home, babe. Seal the deal. The numbers need to look good. I've got a big meeting tonight."

"Tonight? But—"

His cell phone buzzes, and he takes it, mouthing, "Gotta go," as he winks and rushes back inside.

"Why are you in this, Ms. Palmer?" Sin asks as he sidles up to me.

"What?" I scoop my jaw up off the ground, realizing he isn't referring to my conversation with Derrick.

Sin means my work. Of course, he does. His thousand-yard stare roves across the lush grounds, taking it in while not focusing on anything at all.

"The same reason everyone works here. It's personal. We've all been here. Helping family members who need assistance."

He turns, narrowing his eyes. "Family?" The way he says the word is strained, as if he doesn't believe me.

It compels me to share more than I normally would. "My mother had a degenerative condition. There was a lot of pain in her last years of life. I did all I could."

I don't talk about the specifics. How by the time a doctor diagnosed her liver disease, nothing could be done. That it never stopped her from the drugs or the alcohol. Or that despite the unbearable pain she suffered every second of her last days of life, she pushed me away until she was too weak or too tired to put up a fight. There's no way I can explain how you can love a person with all your heart when they seem to hate you with all of theirs, so I don't try.

By the look on Sin's face, I've already given him an uncomfortable amount of information to unpack. So, I wrap it up, quickly finishing. "I did what I could to make her comfortable."

The hard lines of his face soften. "I'm sorry for what you've been through."

"Thank you." The practiced smile I use in times like these emerge, and I nod appreciatively, steering our discussion back where it belongs. On him. And not because Derrick wants me to close the deal, but because this man and his family need me. And that's why I'm here.

"The first steps are never easy," I say as a gentle reminder. "We have different levels of care and service. Can you tell me more about the person who brought you here today?"

He spends another moment looking me up and down, torment storming behind his eyes as they finally settle on mine.

I don't know what to make of it, but situations like these can be delicate. With all my encounters, I'm patient as I let the client drive the discussion, deciding for themselves if they'll tear the bandage off bit by bit, or rip it off all at once.

With an abrupt huff, he steps away, his large, determined strides taking him inside the facility and back toward the lobby. I rush after him, but don't shout out his name or make a scene, not wanting to draw attention from the residents or staff . . . especially Derrick.

Sin wastes no time depositing his visitor badge on the desk, and I nearly break into a jog to catch up to his mile-long stride. When he bolts out the front doors, I'm right behind him, struggling to catch my breath.

"Sin," I say, winded but compassionate. He stops but doesn't face me. "If I've said anything—"

"You haven't."

His reply is so matter-of-fact, I feel silly for suggesting it. So, I reclaim my smile, if only for my own benefit.

"I know trust takes time. My card," I say, holding it out and feeling doubly foolish when he doesn't take it.

Instead, he sneers.

This is the point where others might give up, but I don't. It's the people who push you off the most that are in the most pain. At least, that's the excuse I've always given myself.

He eyes the card, then casts an amused glance to the sky. After an awkward second of silent conversation between him and a few puffy white clouds, he faces me. The hand he places on my shoulder feels paternal. "I don't need your card, Ms. Palmer. The person who brought me here today was you."

Unbuttoning his blazer, he fishes a thin envelope from the inside pocket and hands it to me as a dark car with tinted windows pulls up beside him. "Someone recently told me the first steps are never easy, Ms. Palmer."

A well-dressed chauffeur rushes around to open the back door, and as soon as Sin is seated inside, the man returns to the driver's seat.

The darkened window rolls down, and Sin's smile widens. "Happy birthday."

He slides on a pair of sunglasses as the car rolls away.

CHAPTER 2
Ivy

The black town car makes a left at the end of the drive, disappearing behind a thicket of birch trees, and I'm left there scratching my head. What just happened? I take another look at the plain white envelope in my hand, ready to open it until I notice Derrick. He's been watching from the large window of his office, a practice of his I've come to accept.

There's an intensity to his expression, one I meet with a cheerful smile. It takes him a moment before he returns it, waving me over. Maybe there's a surprise waiting for me. Like gathering the staff over to sing "Happy Birthday." Or an intimate cupcake with a single candle for me to wish upon.

"Everything all right?" Derrick asks as I enter. It's just him and me and the ever-growing clusters of paperwork and folders covering his desk. My hopes for a cupcake are instantly dashed, and it's a wonder he can find anything in the small space. For every new meeting with his accountant, the mounds of paperwork are only getting worse. He closes in from behind me, though the door remains open.

"Yes. He's going to think it over," I say as I slip the envelope into the roomy pocket of my cardigan. I want to remind him that sales aren't made in a day. That trust must be earned. But the irony is enough for me to bite my tongue.

I should tell Derrick about the envelope. For once, trust him. Really let him in. It feels self-sabotaging not to.

As often as I repeat the usual mantra, *I should trust him,* over and over again in my head, I can't deny the parts of my mind and heart that don't . . . and it's not for a lack of trying. Or admitting to myself that I'm damaged goods, the byproduct of an absentee mother and father unknown.

But Derrick is my ticket to a normal relationship, even if things between us have felt a bit uncomfortable lately. It's just a hiccup, one every couple encounters. He's stable. Sweet. A bit of a workaholic, which means I haven't seen him much in the past three weeks. But at least he has a J-O-B, and that should count for something, right?

Still, I can't help but shove the envelope deeper into my oversized pocket, hiding it from both my boyfriend and my boss. No matter how hard I try, distrust slithers between us, threatening to pry us apart.

Let's face it, I have issues, and trust is just the tip of the iceberg.

One of his arms wraps around me. Instead of giving him the usual elbow to the ribs, I nuzzle into him, and it feels . . . nice. Warm and caring and . . . nice. That is, until he releases me. And just like that, I second-guess everything.

Am I like Goldilocks complaining that my man is too nice?

Derrick's shirt is perfectly fitted, the navy blue tapering over his chest and abs before disappearing into his slacks. It looks professional and sexy, though I still prefer his lucky polo. His sweet superstition is that whenever he wears it, luck lands in his lap. As if I was a manifestation of luck.

"Chase another one off?" he says, only half-teasing me.

With his half smile and adorable gaze, maybe he's ready to finally make it official. "Aren't you afraid someone will see us?" I playfully ask, wondering if we can finally stop hiding our status from coworkers and Facebook alike. Be a couple in the actual light of day.

I know I agreed to keep our relationship under wraps, but maybe this is a baby step in the right direction. Hope blooms from deep within my chest that maybe, just maybe, I'm finally learning to trust.

"You're probably right," he says, pulling away to bring us back to a proper boss-employee distance apart. When my frown catches his eye, he lowers his voice. "Hey, it's not forever. Just for now. Meeting you was my destiny."

His sweet words and wink revive my smile, but before I can slip him a kiss, he steps back.

Noticing the envelope, he asks, "What's that?"

It would be so easy to tell him about the tour with Sin. The strange encounter and Sin's bizarre escape. Why can't I take the envelope out and open it with Derrick? Share something, *anything*, with my boyfriend of nearly a year.

I slide the unmarked envelope from my pocket, flipping it aimlessly. "Just a letter."

"I'm running to the post office after work, then I've got a meeting. Need me to mail it for you?"

"I've got it," I say, forcing a smile. "Meeting?" On my birthday?

Derrick has taken several meetings this week away from the office. And another dinner meeting? This can't be good.

His nod is reluctant, and I know when to back off. But I offer him all the support he needs, cuddling Mr. Whiskers against his neck. And like Sin before him, Derrick can't help but crack a smile.

"You and that . . . cat."

I don't know what word he mentally used to fill in the blank between *that* and *cat*, and I don't care. I'm tired of being ruled by my stupid doubts. And they are stupid.

But I tuck Mr. Whiskers back into my pocket, leaning closer to

Derrick's rigid stance. "I need something for luck. I mean, we can't all have a lucky polo."

CHAPTER 3

Ivy

"Table for two. Under Brooke Everly," my best friend says, rescuing me from a birthday dinner for one of mac and cheese.

"You reserved a table?" I ask as we're seated, surprised because we never get a table. We always sit at the bar.

"The strongest they have . . . so we can dance on it. It's your birthday!" She squeals loud enough that absolutely everyone is looking. "And just because your boyfriend has to work doesn't mean we celebrate less. After this, it's karaoke time."

Her elbow nudges mine, and I know she's serious. My throat dangerously tight, I choke down the ball of fear with a few sips of the chilled water our waiter has placed in front of me.

Brooke instantly demands two tequilas. Both for her. "And keep them coming," she tells the waiter.

We've plowed through our first basket of chips as she tosses back her second shot.

"So, let me get this straight," Brooke says as she taps her lip with her index finger. "Some mysterious good-looking guy books a tour with you just to deliver mail and check out your ass?" She slurs the word *ass* and motions for the waiter. "Tell me he at least offered you a lap dance."

"He did not."

"Fucker. So, what did the letter say?"

I shrug. "It's still in my pocket. I got busy, and—"

Her eyes widen. "You didn't want to open it in front of Derrick in case it's a dick pic."

I deadpan. "Who would print out a dick pic?"

"A man who fills the page. You can't open it until after dinner. Birthday present number one."

Laughing, I shrug and dunk another chip into hot, gooey cheese. "Good-looking, yes. But more than twice my age, at least. And we all know twice my age is my hard limit."

"Really? I'll bet he's still hotter than Derrick. You rarely spend the night at his place, and we both know he's never at yours. Plus, he never takes you out. Ever. What kind of eighty-year-old boyfriend is he?"

"For your information, he's thirty. And I'm trying to be supportive as he builds his career."

"For a year? And when's the last time you've had sex?" she shouts, trying to be heard above the lively Mexican music.

Our waiter refills my water, grinning broadly. Sweltering heat rises up my face as I melt into the seat and die of embarrassment. Brooke roars with laughter, planting herself facedown along the bench.

"This coming from a woman whose face is kissing an area where someone's ass has been. After they've eaten their weight in Mexican food."

I ball up my napkin and toss it at my drunk friend's head, which does little good. If anything, it eggs her on, as she moves on from laughter to a perfect whale-song combination of howling, raucous heaving, and silent squeals.

She rubs the flood of hysterical tears from her face before

pointing a finger straight up, conveying how she needs a moment to catch her breath.

Hushed, I lean over. "I've had sex," I say, arguing with the giddy drunk girl. "For your information, I have it regularly."

"Like as regularly as when the salmon swim upstream?"

The waiter brings our food—two shrimp quesadillas for me and a taco salad the size of my Honda Civic for Brooke. I glare at her over the rim of my water glass as she orders a margarita.

"Virgin?" she shouts, having lost all control over the volume of her voice.

I scowl at her until I realize she was talking about a drink. Which actually sounds good.

Turning to the waiter, I ask, "Can you do a pineapple margarita with no alcohol?"

He nods and heads off.

"And more nachos," Brooke hollers after him.

In an instant, her elated happy face drops. Despite the fact that she's a champion lush who can usually out-shot or out-chug any man, I'm almost afraid she's about to be sick.

"You okay?" I ask, ready to rush her to the ladies' room.

She merely points past me, and I turn to see whatever zapped every last drop of happy-go-lucky from her face.

Lo and behold, it's Derrick.

I'm elated that he made it to my birthday celebration after all, until I see he's not in the professional button-down shirt he was wearing earlier at work. And he's not alone.

This version of Derrick looks freshly showered, his hair still damp and curled in a pretty-boy style that actually makes him look younger. Wearing his faded jeans that are my favorite, he's seated at the bar, relaxed as his spread-eagle legs give easy access to let a sloppy blonde slide in between them. She's made herself perfectly comfortable, smoothing her fingers against his chest and shoulders and pretty much all over his lucky fucking polo.

I square my shoulders, and before I know it, I've crossed the length of room, vaguely aware of Brooke huffing, "Shit," as her footsteps stumble behind me. I'm seconds from yanking the blonde by the hair—southern style—when I come to my senses and realize it's not her I'm pissed at.

"Oh, fuck," Derrick says like a dumbass because that's what he is. A worthless, dickless dumbass. He fumbles his way from behind the body of a woman whose perfume smells way too familiar because, like the man she's draped all over, that's also mine.

"Is 'oh, fuck' all you have to say? I guess she's your destiny, too." I frantically search the bar for the biggest drink within reach to toss in his face.

"What's going on?"

When his companion turns to face me, I realize it's none other than his accountant. Which explains all those closed-door and after-work meetings.

"Hey. Iris, right?" she says with the charm of a pole dancer, and now I'm searching the bar for two of the biggest drinks I can find—preferably crammed full of ice.

"Don't make a scene, Ivy," Derrick says calmly like a total idiot. "We're hardly exclusive."

"Excuse me? You're the one who was talking marriage and kids. You're the one who's always asking what cut of diamond I prefer and where our honeymoon should be."

His lips tighten, and his words come out cool. "You can't pin this on me. I need passion. Spontaneity. A woman who will throw caution to the wind. The most I got out of you was your toothbrush."

He means a girl who will throw condoms to the wind. "And that's my fault? You're the one who wanted to keep our relationship on the down-low, and now I know why."

"Grow up. You don't want exclusive. You want to roam fast and free and with whatever guy rolls up. Like Limo-man this afternoon. What was in that envelope he gave you? Cash? A hotel room key?"

"What the fuck, Derrick? No."

At least, I don't think so. Besides, Derrick's so-called accountant is two seconds from sucking him off at the bar, so why am I the one on trial?

Derrick crosses his arms over his chest. "Yeah? Prove it."

He casts an arrogant glance at the pocket of my cardigan because, unlike him, I didn't have time to shower and change clothes before going out. I was actually working.

"I have nothing to prove." Which now looks like I have everything to prove. *Dammit.*

When I feel a tug at the envelope, I whirl around.

Brooke waves Exhibit A suggestively in the air. "And what if she hasn't been cheating on your sorry ass, Dare-dick? What are you willing to wager?"

At least my ride-or-die has my back, though I feel a bead of perspiration trail down the nape of my neck at her suggestion. And since there's no backing down now, I square my shoulders and pray to God that Derrick is wrong.

Derrick waves her off. "It's not like you didn't already destroy the evidence."

"It's still sealed," I say, not certain if I'm making the situation better or worse but not willing to let my friend hang in the wind.

His expression sours. "Fine. What do you want if I'm wrong?"

"Your fucking car, jackass," Brooke says.

Wow. Her balls get all kinds of big after that much tequila. And when my bestie dives in headfirst, demanding his shiny new Mercedes convertible, there's only one thing to say.

"Yeah, Dare-dick," I say, repeating her insult because it's kind of catchy and totally spot-on as he plays fast and loose with Sluts-R-Us over here.

That's not jealousy talking. That's his accountant's cherry red lips now printing a path up another guy's neck before her tongue lands in his ear. It sickens me to remember that you've had sex with everyone your partner's had sex with. Perhaps a few weeks of no action with Derrick is just enough time to avoid a collision course with a round of STDs.

"Fine," he says, bellying up and stepping into my space. I anchor myself in place, ready for whatever he's got. Until he says, "Then if I win, you quit."

"Quit?" I squeak out.

I can't quit. What I do isn't just a job. It's my life. For years, I've cared for every single person in the center. Working evenings. Weekends. Christmas fucking morning. And now he wants me to quit?

Derrick is going too far. I'm not quitting my job over a stupid bet or even a breakup. No way. Not a chance.

I'm about to tell him so when Brooke cracks open the seal of the envelope and pulls out an old-looking photograph. Who in the world has photos anymore?

She flips it around and trombones the square to and from her face in the booze-filled hope of reading it. "Who's Olivia?"

"What?" Carefully, I take the delicate photo from her hand, staring at it hard, as hard as I can. My heart pounds wildly against my ribs, and I stand there, stunned. I blink before I regain my senses and can move.

Brooke slaps the empty envelope on Derrick's chest. "Ivy doesn't need your job. She's an overqualified badass who's tired of taking your shit."

Oh. My. God. Brooke really needs to stop talking now.

"Fuck both of you," Derrick spits out. "I'm not giving you my car."

As Derrick storms off, Brooke shouts after him, "Way to be a bad loser, Dare-dick."

It isn't until she wipes my cheek that I realize I'm crying.

"Hey, don't cry. He doesn't deserve you," she says, stroking my hair.

"It's not that," I say, staring at the image of my mother. At least, I think it's my mother. It's as if Angie's magic wand has brushed alchemist strokes across her image. Her dark curls are thick and full, framing round cherub cheeks and a big, beautiful smile I've never seen her wear. I almost didn't recognize her.

Next to her stands a man I don't know. His dark wavy hair is the perfect crown to his tall stature and confident stance. His lips are a line that barely tips up, and his dimpled chin could have been molded to form mine. But it's his eyes that draw me in. Instantly I want to know him, and it bothers me that I don't.

On the back is a riddle, one I reread again and again . . . and again.

For
Olivia Ann Palmer.

"What is it?" Brooke asks with a side hug that wraps me tight and squeezes out my reply.

"It's me. I'm Olivia Ann Palmer."

CHAPTER 4
Ivy

By the time we get to my apartment, I'm wrung of too many emotions to count. I can't keep up with the barrage of questions Brooke throws at me. Though they're all the same loud ones clanking around in my mind, too. The ones I have no answers for.

Why did Sin have this photograph, and why give it to me now? What made my mom change so much? Was it me? Was I the reason for her change?

And what about the man standing beside her. Who is he? With that chin and those eyes, could he be my father? And even if it is, I can't just ignore nearly twenty years of warning from my mother. Men are evil. Did she mean him? My father was evil? What if every drunken accusation she'd spat about men were really about him?

Or what if none of that was true? My mother stole everything from me. Food. Money. Sanity. A childhood. My trust in men. What if it was all in her head? The angry rantings of a woman too drunk or too confused to understand that all the things that happened to her, she did to herself.

Brooke knocks me from my thoughts, hitting me with another accusatory question. "Are you going by Ivy or Olivia?"

My head drops to my hands. It's hard to explain to someone you've known your whole life that you have a different name.

"And since when is your name Olivia?"

"Birth, obviously." I giggle out a nervous little laugh. It's a memory I've smothered every time it surfaced.

The day I entered first grade, my mom was so intoxicated she couldn't spell Olivia on the brown paper bag she'd packed my lunch in, and it wasn't for lack of trying. The O became as wide as the edges of the bag, and inside that letter was scrawled an *I*, a *V*, and something that passed for a *Y*. The given name on my school records be damned. To absolutely everyone, the drunk scrawls on a brown paper sack were my christening. I was Ivy.

"Are you in witness protection?" Brooke asks in hushed tones.

"I'd tell you, but you know the drill."

"If you tell me, you'd have to kill me. Just remember, this southern girl won't go down easy. Hair and earrings will be pulled."

"I'd expect nothing less," I say, then hold my breath for an uncomfortable stretch.

"Fine," she says with a huff. "Keep your secrets." She frowns. "I'm sorry about Derrick," Brooke says, her bright green eyes sweetly compassionate.

"Me, too," I reply with a shrug because the truth is, I'm not as sorry as I thought I'd be. Derrick was never overly affectionate in public, and I never pressed the issue. I foolishly thought he wanted to maintain a professional boundary. Unless, of course, you're his accountant.

"The truth is," I begin, "I don't blame him."

Brooke's eyebrow lifts in disbelief. "Like, you don't blame him. Now, let's go key his car?"

"No, like there was something missing, and I felt it, too."

"Was it his teeny-tiny dick?"

I giggle. "That, too." I sigh, deflating. "It's exactly what he said. Passion. Spontaneity. I need that, too. And how about a little adventure and romance. Like straight out of a steamy novel. Where is that hot god ready to sweep me off my feet?"

"Um, every woman wants that."

"I'd settle for just one night."

"Yes! We need to manifest a smoking-hot rebound god. And I'll take one, too." I give her a sideways glance. "Just throwing that out in the universe."

"As much as I'd love to be seduced by a stranger, I have a feeling this guy is about to take up all my free time." I flip the photo in my fingers.

Brooke scoots to one side of the sofa, patting the cushion beside her. I cuddle into my half of the couch, snuggling into the blanket as we both search the image for clues. "Who are you?" I whisper to the man captured in the shot, wishing so hard the picture of my mom would come alive and tell me.

"What's that?" Brooke asks, pointing to a stone plaque on the building behind them. Though the background is blurred, I can just make it out.

"It looks like a really big upper-case letter D." Noticing the swirl of a tail, I add, "A fancy one. Which might be helpful if I knew anything else at all because asking Alexa to tell me more about the letter D might take all night."

"No, not that. This. The newspaper." Brooke points to the one rolled up beneath his arm. Grabbing her phone, she snaps a shot, then zooms out the image of the newspaper's headline. The letters come into focus. "Chicago," she squeals excitedly. "It says Chicago. And there's a date."

The date feels illusive and surreal, and I recalculate it in my head more than a few times. Six months. This was six months before I was born. I'm looking at myself, hidden deep inside the still slim belly of my mother. And the man beside her is so much bigger in that moment.

For so long, Brooke was the closest thing to family that I had. Her home was always too full of parents and siblings and so much laughter my heart ached for the glimmers of it I stole by her side. But the more I stare at the photo, the more I wonder. Is there a family out there that's mine?

"Oh, my God, I have a brilliant idea," Brooke announces.

"Your brilliant ideas usually involve illegal fireworks or bail money."

"Shhh." She shushes me. Then, she jumps off the couch, her dramatic hands hushing a non-existent crowd. I arch a brow. "Two words," she says, holding two fingers in the air. "Aunt Grace."

A smile warms my face because I love Brooke's Aunt Grace. She's warm cookies and tea, smothering you with endless hugs and the scent of juniper berries. I'm not ashamed to admit of all Brooke's family, Aunt Grace is my favorite. "Ooh, I could really use her sweet potato pie right now. Is she coming to visit?"

"Better! You're going to visit her." Brooke snatches the photo from my fingers, holding it up to my face. "In Chicago."

I couldn't let go of the thought. Chicago. For hours, the romantic fantasy of me escaping my comfortable lifestyle for a fast-paced adventure of a big city had me awake. Brooke is the wild one. I'm the wallflower. These are our roles. Hence the fully-packed duffle lying on the bed beside me. Brooke had it neatly packed and ready to go a Chicago-second after deciding I was going. But I'm not going.

Am I?

I sigh an exhausted breath as I weigh the options. Here, I have people I care about. A life. A job ... unless Derrick took Brooke's drunken rant at face value. And even if he didn't, is that what I want? Working with him day in and day out? Because between my simmering anger and his lack of self-awareness or people skills, I feel an impending kick to his nuts in no time.

I wrestle with the comforter, trying to find that perfect spot that turns my mind all the way off. As quickly as sleep closes in, it's chased away again with images of a tall, dark stranger with piercing eyes and so many features like mine. My mother's hair was midnight dark with thick, tight curls. She never had answers for the long, sable wavy lengths that draped down my back. Wrapping several strands through my fingers, I twirl away the pain. My hair was just another piece of me she seemed to loathe.

Was it because of him?

I grab my phone and open my email, posturing my fingers for an executive decision I might regret. Without overthinking it any longer, I type five words to the man, and the life, I've been tethered to.

Go fuck yourself. I quit.

It was a hasty move, I admit, even for me. But it felt damn good in the moment. Fingers crossed I've hit rock bottom, and the only way to go is up. With the two biggest decisions of my life out of the way, I settle into sleep, knowing this brings me closer to the one man who's always been out of reach.

CHAPTER 5

Ivy

"Come here and give your Aunt Grace a hug." I love that she calls herself *my* Aunt Grace. I love it even more that her arms are wrapped around me before I could even say "hi." Her bear hug is tight and warm and relaxes all my apprehensions and doubts, filling me with the reassurance that everything will be all right.

I've barely stepped a foot inside her home when the aroma of sweet potato pie hits me. "Mmm, something smells amazing," I say with a silent commitment to only have one slice tonight. But honestly, after driving for twelve hours with nothing but a bag of Fritos and gas station roller food, who am I kidding? All bets are off.

She pulls me away, locking her big blue-green eyes with mine. "Brooke told me about your breakup. I'm so sorry," she says, frowning.

"I'm not," I say with renewed conviction. "New day. New life."

Her soft hands cup my cheeks. "Good. He would only stand in the way of you and your amazing adventure." Her eyes are alive with delight. "Come on." Her arm loops around mine, tugging me in. "I've got tea and pie and have to know what's pulling my shy little Ivy-vine from home."

Ivy-vine. I forgot she used to call me that. My smile grows remembering how much I'd cling to her every time she was in arms-reach. I relax, knowing she doesn't mind in the slightest that I still cling to her now.

We head to the kitchen, where the seating area is cozy, with sunlight pouring through lace sheers at the open picture window. The cabinets are a perfect country-white, and the bouquet of fresh daisies makes me smile. As soon as I sit, a large slice of pie is set before me along with a mug of tea. The mug has a whole pie pictured at the bottom, with a caption that reads, "You want a piece of me?"

Bite after bite, I share everything that's happened in the past day and a half and show her the photo. Aunt Grace shines a skeptical eye between me and the photo as she holds it to my face. I bite my lip nervously. "Well? See any resemblance?"

She wrinkles her face. "Hard to say. I always thought you and I looked alike … right here." She taps the tip of my nose, then adjusts her glasses to take a better look at the image of my mom and the man beside her. "That looks familiar."

I swallow my bite. "What does?"

"That letter D. Hang on." From a stack of magazines and newspapers, she pulls out the classified section. "Here." On the front page of the classifieds is a job announcement, with a letter D as a logo. Side by side, the Ds are identical.

"Why were you reading the classifieds? Are you looking for a job?" I thought she was retired.

Aunt Grace waves me off. "I don't have children or cats. I read everything I can get my hands on." She refocuses on the ad. "Help wanted. Caretaker."

"Like a gardener?"

"I don't think so." She sips her tea and continues. "More like a jack-of-all-trades. Running errands. Tidying up. In-home care."

She looks up at me. "Does that mean they want someone to live there?"

I shrug a shoulder, mumbling, "Maybe," as I take a large piece of pie into my mouth. I swallow. "Sometimes that's code for working with someone who may be elderly or disabled." Not unlike the ads we used to place at Sparrow Wellness. "But what does the D stand for?"

She fingers down the ad. "Oh, it's at the D'Angelo Towers building downtown." Her eyes beam with delight. "It's one of the biggest skyscrapers in Chicago. Maybe if you show that picture to the front desk, they can help you."

"Maybe."

Neatly, she folds the paper in half and sets it next to me. "Give me your hand."

Her fingers wiggle expectantly as I lay my hand in hers. Aunt Grace has always believed herself to be somewhat of a mystic, and palm reading is just the start. I'm sure the room she has me in is dotted with clear quartz and purple crystals, and the Tarot cards can't be far.

Despite her track record for predicting that one day I'd be a stately queen in a lavish castle, butterflies flutter wildly in my belly as I await her premonition.

"Oh, look at this," she says with a suggestive lift in her voice.

I lean in, hushing my words. "What do you see?"

"This." She traces a finger from one side of my hand upward. "This is your love line. Love is in the air, sweet girl. Love is in the air."

Considering the hellacious breakup I just had, I shut down the defensive eye roll and play along. "Really? Because Brooke ordered me a smoking hot rebound god. Can you see how far out he is? Like, is he on the delivery truck now?"

"Soon, baby girl. Very soon." Aunt Grace winks with a frisky giggle.

CHAPTER 6
Ivy

Morning gave me enough time to get my ducks in a row. D'Angelo Tower shouldn't take too long to get to. My cell pings, and I see the text from my bank. It isn't good.

FRAUD ALERT. SUSPICIOUS ACTIVITY. CARD LOCKED

Keeping my cool, I call to explain that I've been traveling, and it's really me that's been using my card. When the agent goes through the necessary security measures to confirm my identity, he begins to list off the transactions, and I agree line by line. But when we get to the charges in Illinois, it all goes wrong.

"Eight-hundred and sixty dollars at Neiman Marcus in Chicago."

"What? No!"

"One thousand dollars at Saks Fifth Avenue in Chicago."

"Oh, my God. I don't have that kind of money." The room spins as panic consumes me.

"It's all right," the agent says, calming me a little. "There are a few more on here."

"A few more?" I'm on the verge of hyperventilating.

"Don't worry. We monitor spending behavior. And we'll work with the stores to investigate. In the meantime, we'll remove them from your account."

My breathing slows. "Really?"

"Yes. Can you check if the card is in your possession?"

I check my wallet. I thumb through every pocket of it, over and over. My search comes up empty. "It's gone. I remember putting it in the pump." My first gas station in Chicago. "I paid at the pump. Maybe I dropped it. I went to use the bathroom. When I returned, a black car was waiting to use the pump, so I hurried to free up the space."

I only remember the car because if a car could glare with impatience, this one did.

Again, his tone is even, settling my nerves as he tries to make me feel better. "Even if you had it, it's compromised. With it gone, you can also file a police report. And we'll send you a new one."

Crap. That means I have exactly five hundred dollars to my name, the extent of my savings.

"Can you confirm the address we have for you on file."

"I'm not in North Carolina. I'm visiting a friend in Chicago. I'm not sure how long I'll be here," I say because honestly, going home has always been my safety net. The Windy City isn't exactly a long-term plan.

"We can hold off on sending you a card until you're sure. Or we can overnight it for a small fee."

When he tells me the fee for overnighting it, I decline. With Aunt Grace, I don't have to worry about a hotel room. But I can't rely on her for everything, and every penny counts since at the present time, I'm unemployed. And this is Chicago. The twelfth most expensive city in the US, according to Alexa.

"Is there anything else I can do for you, Ms. Palmer?" he asks.

Not unless you can find my father. "No, thank you," I say politely through a fog of disappointment. I hadn't planned to use my small line of credit, but it was my backup plan if I needed to stay longer. As it is, my options are to stay until my savings disintegrate, or find a job.

I grab the newspaper and flip it right side up. They're looking to hire, and I need employment. It wouldn't hurt to drop by. Check out the job, and while I'm at it, see if anyone recognizes him from his picture.

And just like that, the stranger in the photo has my attention. Mom never talked about my father, if this man is my father, except to say he was a bad man. But that never kept me from wondering about him. That secret childhood fantasy of him showing up out of the blue and knowing me by nothing more than the look in my eyes because that's how connected we are. Hope begins to bloom in my chest.

But the longer I stare at him the longer I wonder. What if that connection isn't there? What if he doesn't miss me? Or want me? Or . . . love me?

I've always believed deep down in my soul that he would be someone that I would love. But what if Mom was right? What if he is a bad man—an evil man—and all this time, she kept him out of my life for a reason?

Or, what if it's *me* who doesn't love *him*? What if I can't love him because I can't trust him . . . because how can you trust someone who would give you up and let you go?

I need answers. And right now, those answers are in D'Angelo Tower.

By the time I'm done filing the police report and feeling absolutely foolish for bringing up the black car at the gas station, my afternoon is shot. I try to race to D'Angelo Tower, but it isn't until I'm in the middle of the heart of Chicago that I realize most of the downtown is bumper-to-bumper congestion. And there is no parking anywhere. Welcome to the big city.

D'Angelo Tower is a monument of glass that takes up an entire city block. One which I've circled three times already. But when a swanky town car pulls out from the front of the building, I pull in and park.

I blow out an anxious breath and glance again at the photo, though there's no need. I've memorized every line and curve of both their faces. But looking at them helps steel my nerves.

I take another look at myself in the rearview mirror, mostly to see if crazy-hair lady has it under control. Instead of focusing on getting my thick waves in check, a chill pricks down my spine as the mirror reveals a black sedan parked several cars back. It reminds me of the one from the gas station. The one that waited behind me even with other pumps open. Not that that means anything. Maybe their gas tank was only on that side.

Nevertheless, I squint hard. There's no way to make out the license plate from here, not that it would make a difference. It's not like I memorized it. I remind myself that black cars are common. And the odds of the same car following me after they grabbed my credit card are a billion to one. Impossible, right?

A knock at the window startles me. A policeman.

Relieved, I release a sigh and roll down the window. "Everything all right, Officer?"

"Sorry, miss. I didn't mean to startle you. But you can't park here."

He points to the sign just above my car. The bold red lettering makes the RESERVED—NO PARKING really stand out. I have no excuse.

"There's public parking in several garages." He points up ahead, and a big blue sign with a P is a stone's throw away.

The name on his tag aptly reads FRIENDLY, which makes me grin.

"Is your name really Friendly?"

He nods, and his smile widens, creasing his face in a charming way that seems to suit him. "Guilty as charged."

Out of options, I plead my case, clasping my hands together because the only alternative in this situation is to beg. "Please. I swear, I'll only be twenty minutes. Half an hour at most. I promise you I wouldn't ask if it wasn't very, very important." Because where I'm from, NO PARKING sign or not, half the time I can at least get a small reprieve to rush in and out if I ask nicely.

He leans in, genuine as he says, "I believe you. Very, very important. But is it very, very important enough to get your car towed? Not by me, mind you. I'd never do that to a fellow Southerner." He turns up his drawl. Texas, I think. "But there's a whole team whose very existence seems to rest on how happy they can keep all the grumpy executives. I'm pretty sure there's a running bet on how fast the tow truck shows up. I've seen it happen about a dozen times this week. But the garages aren't too far."

Frowning, I can see the big parking sign from here, and the words under it. CREDIT CARD ONLY.

"Hey," he says, his once-over of my well-worn car giving him pause. Obviously, I'm a hard-luck case. "If you need cash for the garage—"

A tangle of appreciation and embarrassment swirls inside me as he fishes his wallet from the back pocket of his pants, ready to hand over a little cash.

"No, it's not that. I have cash, but my credit card was stolen this morning," I say, and his worried frown prompts me to add, "I already filed a report."

He wrinkles his brow. "New card coming?"

I nod, not bothering to explain that it will be . . . once I figure out where to send it to.

I take another glance at the rearview mirror, letting idle curiosity, or anxiety, get the best of me. The ominous black car is gone, replaced by a brightly colored delivery truck.

My sigh of relief is silly as I turn back to the officer. "I've circled the building several times already, trying to find anywhere that takes cash."

"Oh, no problem. Go past the first three garages. The last one on the right takes cash."

Grateful, I nod.

"And you might wanna get a move on," Officer Friendly says, "because the Tower closes soon."

It's barely four. "But I thought it didn't close until six."

"Renovations. But they'll have regular hours tomorrow."

The cop gives me a reassuring salute and taps the hood of the car, the universal symbol for *move it along*.

My stomach knots when I recheck the time, determined that if I don't get there today, I'll come back tomorrow. Though the thought of entering this kind of traffic of my own free will is enough to make me never, ever want to drive here again.

I head out into traffic, being careful not to hit the random pedestrian as Officer Friendly continues waving back. The parking garage I'm looking for may be less than two blocks away, but with traffic moving slower than molasses, I'll be lucky to get back by New Year's.

My heart pounding, I monitor the rush-hour gridlock, and the many pedestrians taunting me as they proceed to kick my ass, gaining by leaps and bounds along the sidewalk. Yeah, I'd be fast, too, if I hopped the curb and used the sidewalk. Tempting. Very tempting.

A year later, I finally make it past the three upscale parking garages that only take credit cards, finding a sketchy-looking parking garage and a questionably sober attendant who does indeed take cash. The sign on his booth reads NO ATTENDANT PAST SIX.

Note to self. Get back to my car well before dark.

CHAPTER 7
Leo

"Seriously?"

I stare at the small beat-up car hogging my space as well as the police officer standing beside it. How long is this going to take? It's been a while since our paths have crossed, but I'd spot Ross Friendly anywhere, and clearly, the son of a bitch sees me.

True to his name, I watch as he charms the pants off whoever's got his attention. Insistent, I wave my hands frantically, mouthing, "Hurry up." He leans in, continuing what I assume to be a marathon round of tail chasing.

Not that it matters. Honestly, I could sit here and watch this flirt-fest all day, because the all-nighter waiting for me isn't going anywhere. In the next half-hour, the building will undergo a major upgrade of all security systems. Heat sensors. Weapons sensors. Facial recognition. Everyone who enters will be tagged and cataloged like we own them. And in so many ways, we do.

Who they are. What they do. Where they live. How many children they have. How many lovers. Gathering pieces of information like a collection of knives. Weapons to be used at our will. I have one job to do. Protect the D'Angelos at all costs. And I've become damned good at it, even if deep down I know it'll cost me my soul.

With more blood on my hands than I'll ever admit to, and my body chained to a suit and tie to ensure my public persona is squeaky clean, most days I'd rather be sucking back beers on a beach in Mexico. But I gave a dead man my vow, so here I remain.

An eternity later, the small Honda with North Carolina plates pulls into traffic, making way for my blue Mercedes to claim the spot. By the cheesy grin on Ross's face, it's easy to romanticize a life where the biggest fucking thing on my agenda is picking up chicks.

I step out. "Just going to let that car go? What kind of beat cop are you?"

I don't waste any time giving Ross Friendly hell. What are SEAL swim buddies for? When he does a crisp about-face, I meet his sharp salute with my own before wrapping him in a long overdue bro-hug.

"How long has it been?" he asks.

"Too long."

An awkward silence stretches between us, and I swallow hard before he says it. The reason I've shut myself away from Ross and people and life. Life's overrated.

"I was so sorry to hear about Lori."

Just hearing her name squeezes my heart, and for a second, I can't breathe. But then the next breath comes, like it has for the past two years. Crushing me all over again, a ten-thousand-pound weight slowly wringing the life from me.

After clearing my throat, I say what I always say. The practiced, "Thanks," comes out numb and emotionless. Time to change the subject. "You spent a lot of time handing out a simple ticket. She must have been pretty."

His chuckle is genuine, the one of a man enjoying life. Like I used to. "No ticket, and she was. The kind of pretty that had me reaching for my wallet to cover the cost of her parking."

"Damn. Tell me you at least got her phone number."

Ross is unusually shy, shaking his head. "We're not all smooth talkers like you."

He means like I used to be. That eternity ago when I cared enough to ask a woman out. When was the last time? I'm lost in my own thoughts until a piece of his conversation piques my interest, dragging me back to the discussion.

"Seems her credit card was stolen this morning," Ross says, "but she had cash. Just couldn't find the cash garage."

My face drops. "You didn't. You sent her to the cash garage?"

Ross shrugs. "Pretty? Yes. Worth me handing my credit card to? No. Remember, I'm a magnet for gals who are sweet but psycho." An urgent announcement emanates from his radio, and he tugs it from the high corner of his chest. "On my way."

Seeing his apology brewing, I raise a hand, stopping him and waving him off. "Get out of here. Help another damsel in distress. One sweeter. Less psycho."

Ross nods with a smile and steps away, then stops. "Let's get together. It's been too long."

A night of reminiscing sounds like a fresh hell I'll never be ready for. And the enforcer to a notorious mob family sitting down with Chicago's finest? Worst plan ever.

"Sounds good," I say, lying with enough conviction that he nods and heads out.

I can't help sending him off with a small prayer that he'll be safe. It's a little weird, worrying about a six-foot-three-inch full-grown man strapped inside a Kevlar vest with a Glock 42 by his side, but I do.

I shake off the unexpected meeting, the taste of encountering humanity again still fresh. It's something I don't need or want. What I do want is to drown myself in work until exhaustion drives me to sleep.

The tower is emptier than usual, making it easy to assess the last of the people who will need to clear out.

I head up to the security suites on the tenth floor. It's a low enough floor so we can put eyes on the streets surrounding the tower, and high enough up to enjoy a view.

As usual, my team is a well-oiled machine. To upgrade the security for a skyscraper this size would take weeks. But most of the heavy lifting has been staged ahead of time, ensuring that all the tasks that must be done tonight are assembly-lined and ready to go. I'm not even sure why I'm here.

Apparently, my team feels the same way as one of those smart-asses has left a copy of a cooking magazine front and center on my desk. Well, joke's on them because that photo on the cover of Grilled Cheese with Bacon-Date Jam speaks to me, moves me on a deeply spiritual level. Keeping an eye on the monitors, I devote most of my brain to the required shopping list for an escape with the only woman left on earth who truly sees me. Rachael Ray.

Somehow, the thrill of preparing a lavish grilled cheese for one releases a pang of loneliness instead of hunger, and any appetite I've managed to work up fades into emptiness. I set the magazine back down as memories of laughter over a bottle of wine and a burnt grilled cheese leave me empty and cold.

Food can't save me. Friends can't save me. But work? Yes. Work will keep me busy and focused. And for the most part, sane.

I notice a person entering the building and note the time. Three minutes before we should be shut down. Daniels enters with a brisk knock. Before he says a word, I reply. "I see her. Why is she here?"

"The front desk says she's here for a job application. She's up here from North Carolina. I'll let them know she needs to come back tomorrow."

"No," I say, needing to do something more with my time than quote-unquote supervise. "I'll head down. I can check on the progress on the ground floor."

Rather than the elevator, I opt for the stairs. Not just because ten floors give me a solid few minutes of cardio, but because I need to talk with my boss, and it annoys the shit out of me when I lose signal in an elevator.

"Well, boss, you're S.O.L." The disappointment in my voice is unavoidable.

Even through the phone, I know Smoke is frowning, the furrow of his brow as apparent as if he were standing right in front of me, giving me his usual broody scowl. "Are you telling me that nothing ties my father's disappearance to the Antonovs?"

"Nothing concrete."

"I'm not asking for a preponderance of evidence we can use in a court of law, Leo."

"And it's been four-and-a-half years. By now, we should start hearing whispers, but instead, everyone is clamming up. Trust me, I'm ready to start plucking people off the street and handling this the old-fashioned way, but you want information, not a war."

"Maybe I want both."

"And maybe I want a normal fucking life, but we don't always get what we want, Smoke." Fuck, why did I say that?

I can feel the energy between us shift, and it morphs in a way that already twists my gut with discomfort. Smoke is my boss. I am his employee. Never mind that the lines blur between us more times than not or that I'd take a fucking bullet for the bastard. It's coming. I know it's coming, and I pinch the bridge of my nose and release a meditative exhale.

"You, uh, want to talk about it?" he asks in such a brotherly way, my steps stop.

Do I want to talk about it? He's asking because apparently, he's forgotten the dick between my legs. I'm a guy. Guys don't talk. Why would we want to talk about anything when raising an electric fence between us is so much easier? "Nothing a little Muay Thai won't cure."

He drops it, quickly changing the subject. "Don't forget. I need you here tomorrow. All day."

I resume making my way down the last two flights of stairs. "Interviewing nurses? Look, it's none of my business, but she doesn't need more medical care. She just needs a little TLC." The instant I say it, I want to suck the words right back in.

"Not a nurse. A caretaker. Maybe the best of both worlds. She can't be alone. You saw that cut on the inside of her arm." My eyes shut. "Maybe it was a cooking accident. Maybe not." Smoke's sigh is long, and I share his pain. "I'm about to be gone more and more. And so are you."

The man may be the biggest pain in my ass on a daily basis, but my boss has a point. Taking down the Bratva syndicate, soldier by soldier, means all that pent-up energy I'm suffocating in is about to evaporate.

"Someone needs to look out for Trinity," he says, and I know he's right.

"But hiring some rando off the street isn't exactly smart. This is more than vetting the right candidate and checking out their background, Smoke. They need to be prepared for the type of life they'll be signing up for." The life I signed up for.

"That's your job," my boss says, pointing out how my job description expands on a fairly regular basis. "They'll report directly to you. Clear your calendar for tomorrow. You'll be interviewing them with me. So, you'll have a say."

"How many candidates?"

"Seventeen."

Christ, that'll take all goddamn day. But this is Trinity, and nothing comes before her. I didn't just make that promise to her father. I made it to myself. And it's not like I've got anything better to do.

At the ground floor, I step closer to the front desk. Notes of citrus and vanilla wrap around me as I close in on the woman handing back what I assume is a job application. The strange thing is a second later, she's not speaking to the attendant, Judith, and she's not preparing to leave. She's just standing there, frozen, as she stares aimlessly at the wall.

It gives me a minute to take a good look at her as I approach. Blessed with luscious dark curls, full decadent lips, and brown eyes I could lose myself in for days, she has skin the color of cappuccino, and just as creamy. I feel her pull like the sun, hand-delivered to me like a gift. And there's nothing I can do but soak her in.

She, on the other hand, is in a sudden rush to leave. Maybe Judith gave her the boot, though I doubt it with her sweet, eager-to-please demeanor that she was hired for.

In her haste, she rushes toward the lobby door, far too preoccupied with getting her things together to notice anything at all around her. Let alone me.

I see her trajectory but don't move, though I'm genuinely surprised when her soft body crashes into mine . . . because it excites me. And nothing excites me nowadays.

"Sorry. Excuse me," she says before hurrying outside.

I watch her rush out the door and drop her purse. One that, like the car that hogged my parking space, has seen better days. The strap is a thread or two from snapping, and I'm pretty sure the zipper doesn't work.

As soon as it hits the ground, I'm right behind her. Out of her bag spills twenty after twenty, several hundred dollars by my estimation, and a photograph. Despite the breeze picking up, she doesn't go for the cash that's about to be swept along the streets of Chicago. Both her hands latch onto the photo, so I focus on the cash.

"Hang on," I tell Smoke as I scoop up the money. Calming the panic in her face, I hand it all back. "Here you go."

Breathing hard, she clutches the photo to her chest like an infant rescued from the Titanic. Her expression is sincere and appreciative, with a smile I'd give anything to taste. "Thank you.

You'd think I'd be more careful. This is my lifeline since my credit card was stolen."

Her credit card was stolen. This is definitely the Honda from North Carolina.

Ross was wrong. This woman isn't pretty. She's breathtaking.

She tucks the money and photo back in her bag, and this fresh-faced girl who isn't my type whatsoever smiles wider. I scan her face quickly, memorizing it.

"Anytime," I say.

A long beat passes between us as a gust of wind whips her thick black curls from her smooth skin and angelic face, and there's no hiding it. I'm staring. And blocking her way. The second she bites that plump lower lip, I have two choices—get out of this nice woman's way or follow the trail of her teeth with my tongue.

Reluctantly, I step aside. She hesitates for a second before taking a step. Like there's something on her mind. Something she wants. Something she needs.

God, please let it be something she needs.

But the struggle behind her expression wanes as she takes another glance at the tower behind me. "Thanks again," she says and heads off.

As she moves away, the warmth and glow of her presence cools, and I realize there was a reason Ross didn't get her digits. It's not that we have no game, though I definitely don't. It's that the woman stuns you right out of rational thought.

Fuck, it's a miracle I wasn't blithering and drooling. Or maybe that's why she left. Am I drooling?

Hell, she shouldn't have walked away. She should have run. Because here I am, still watching her retreat as my boss soaks up every fucking word.

"Hey," I finally have the presence of mind to say. "You still there?"

Smoke chuckles. "Are you kidding? I wouldn't miss this for the world. The real question is, what the hell are you still doing there?"

41

It might be a fair question, but it doesn't feel fucking fair. "I don't do relationships."

"Then don't propose. One foot in front of the other. Get her name. Maybe share a meal. Think of it as shore leave."

I'm half a second from telling my boss—my best friend—to go fuck himself. But I bite my tongue and exhale all my frustration. Just like my SEAL training, my therapist, and twenty hours a week of YouTube yoga videos have me doing.

"One date won't kill you," he says.

It isn't me I'm worried about.

I walk back inside, irritated that Judith has managed to slip out in the minutes I've been away. Whatever paperwork this girl filled out is now locked up. I could break into the cabinet. Or I could get a life and resume my work. No matter which one I choose, I don't need to keep Smoke on the phone. "I have to go."

"Do what you gotta do, Leo. But be here bright and early. At eight."

"In the morning?" I scoff.

Not wasting his breath with a reply, Smoke simply hangs up, knowing I'll be ten minutes early.

Determined to get my mind off whatever the hell happened just now, I glance at the wall the woman was looking at. The life-like image of Antonio D'Angelo looks down at me, and it's enough to nudge me back to work.

For two hours, I check up on a team of reconnaissance engineers who don't exactly need adult supervision. It isn't until I take a glance out the window at the street below that a small concern surfaces. "Daniels," I holler out the open door.

"Sir," he says, entering.

"How long has she been sitting there?" I point to the girl who'd been in the lobby not two hours ago. From across the street, she's made herself comfortable on the steps of the corporate plaza. Daniels doesn't come to the window. No doubt, the team has been monitoring her.

"Since she left the building."

"Hmm." I frown, checking my watch. No credit card. What if she has nowhere to go?

I shake my head because, at the very least, she has a car. It's in the crappy cash lot Ross sent her to. She moves something to her lips. "What's she eating?"

"I believe it's a Twinkie, sir."

I eye him skeptically. "They still make those?"

Unsure, he shrugs. "Want us to get rid of her?" Daniels asks. If I say yes, no doubt I'll never see her again, and I don't want that. At least, my cock doesn't. Considering that it's been a while since it's had something to say about anyone, I heed the instant throb as I watch her finish the cream-filled cake.

"No. I'll take care of it."

Daniels gets back to the team, and I head out.

The easiest way to approach her is directly. Out the front door and straight over. But seeing me coming gives her time to think up a reason for why she's there, and the truth comes faster when questions aren't expected. I can't put my finger on why my guard is up. But it is.

Or is this me? I feel myself walking a fine line between obsessing over a beautiful stranger and tattooing SUSPECT across her gorgeous ass. Is it too much to ask that she be both?

I leave out the side exit, cross the street, and quiet my steps to observe her for a minute. What am I doing here? She isn't doing anything. And anyone on my team could've looked into this. And yet, here I stand. Gawking at her like a starved wolf, I'm half a second from springing wood right here for all of Downtown Chicago to see.

I'm indecisive, and I'm never indecisive. In fact, I'm usually the opposite. Brash. Impulsive. Every so often, hotheaded and moody . . . especially when the next season of *The Bachelorette* is taking forever to start.

Don't judge. I'm free to be a hopeless romantic in the sanctuary of my own home.

By the time the whirlwind of citrus and vanilla wafts around me again, I clear my throat.

Startled, she jumps in place.

I lift my hands innocently. "Just checking if you're all right."

"Oh. I was just thinking." She pauses, studying my face. "Do I know you?"

Pointing to the entrance of the lobby, I reply, "You ran into me earlier."

Her shoulders relax as a smile brightens her somber expression. "Right."

I take a seat beside her, both to better understand what's grabbed her attention for so long and to get closer because apparently, my body has a mind of its own. "It's a beautiful building," I say honestly.

"Do you know much about it?" she asks, and as soon as she faces me, I see it. A smudge of Twinkie cream on her lower lip.

And because I'm a lunatic, I lift my hand to her face. "Stay still." *What the hell am I doing?*

Her eyes widen as my thumb dusts her lower lip, but she does as I say. She doesn't move. And fuck. Now I'm hard.

The trace of a blush warms her, and for the first time in a long time, I feel it. A spark. Something that jolts me back to the land of the living.

Her gaze falls to my mouth, and mine drops to hers, and we sit there. And with both of us staring, it's not awkward at all, right? "It was erected in the nineties," I say, watching as her eyes widen even more.

Shyly, she moves her gaze to the tower, and I continue rattling off facts and figures like a tour guide. "At one thousand feet tall and with one hundred stories, it's not only one of the tallest buildings in Chicago but in the US. Now, your turn."

"My turn?" When her full lips pull into a small smile that lights up her face, I quell the suspicions that nag at me.

"To answer a question." I point my chin to the building ahead of us. "What has you so fascinated?"

She ponders my question, and I'm in no hurry as she bites her lower lip, searching the floors of the looming tower for an answer. This time, I take a good long look at her.

I wasn't imagining it. She's stunning. Her lips are luscious, her scent alluring, and her demeanor absolutely adorable. But I think it's her sadness that captivates me the most. Something her smile can't completely hide. "I think my future might be in that building," she says. She must mean the job. I wonder which one she was applying for.

"But," she adds, "I'm not sure I'm ready to face my future." She turns to me, and her big eyes search mine. "What would you do?"

"Considering I don't know you at all or have any idea what we're talking about, when in doubt, take the red pill."

Her brow lifts. "Huh?" And then she scoots a little further away. "I'm not into drugs."

I chuckle. "It's from *The Matrix*. When confronted with the choice to face the truth head-on, no matter how unsettling, or to stay blissfully ignorant, choose truth."

Her face twists with uncertainty. "What if I don't like the truth? What if the truth changes everything? And not for the better?"

There's that single silvery curl near her temple that I want to wrap around one finger, and a trace of a southern accent that hits me right in the dick.

I can do a date. No commitments. No one's talking forever. It's just. One. Date.

I stand and button my blazer. "Let's go."

"Go?"

"We can't have a deep conversation without a drink." I extend a hand and she takes it, letting me help her to her feet.

"I don't drink," she says, the tease of an invitation in her smile as she begins walking slowly away.

Not one to give up, I fall into step beside her. "Dinner?" I say, sweetening my offer.

"I've already eaten," she says in a feeble attempt to decline.

I take the crumpled Twinkie wrapper from her hand. "I can think of better things to satisfy your appetite." Her slow stroll stops, and she faces me with a no-nonsense pout that's too perfect for words. "I mean food."

"Tempting. But I'm not sure how long I'll be in Chicago. I don't think it's a good idea."

Her hesitation gives me pause. "Husband?"

"No."

"Boyfriend?"

"No."

"Girl . . . friend?" I ask, drawing out the word salaciously, oddly hopeful because, for the first time in a long time, I'm having fun.

Her slow stroll stops again, and that perfect pout turns into a frown. "Why is girl-on-girl action such a thing for men?"

Shrugging, I pocket my hands and lean in, because now I'm curious. "Is that a no?"

Her head shakes with the sort of denial that tells me she's having fun, too. "No."

This time, when she breaks away, her steps are faster. Purposeful. It's not a challenge to keep pace with her, and our strides line up.

"Then have dinner with me."

"I can't."

"Because you're not attracted to me?"

"Right. Because I have an aversion to Calvin Klein models with seductive charm."

"Funny, I don't hear a convincing objection."

"Sorry, Cal. You're exactly what I don't need right now."

I stop cold. "And what's that?"

She continues walking without me, rushing away as she hollers back. "A commitment."

The more this woman pushes me away, the more my dick has to have her. I take several steps after her, muttering under my breath, "That's my line."

It takes a second to gain speed on the woman who just slipped into one of the seediest parking garages in the city. I don't even know her, but in an instant, I want to protect her. Especially from the scumbag who just crawled out from around the side of the garage and followed her in. I doubt his intentions are as pure as mine, and mine are a stone's throw from involving rope and a blindfold.

By the time I catch up, she's clutching her bag for dear life, terror splayed across her face. I pull out my weapon just as the purse strap snaps in their little tug-of-war.

Before he can make a move or take off, my Glock is trained straight between the lowlife's eyes. "I suggest you hand the purse back to the lady."

The idiot takes a second to think it through, and reluctantly does as I've asked before raising his hands in surrender.

"You all right?" I ask the woman.

She blinks frantically for a second before nodding, so I turn to the man.

"Good news. She's uninjured. You get to live." As I wave my Glock toward the exit, my lip curls with satisfaction. "Run, asshole. Before I change my mind."

Wisely, he takes off, and I turn my attention back to the woman. With pure adrenaline pumping through my veins, I restrain the need to take her up against the side of her car.

Her brow pinches. *Did she just read my thoughts?*

"Why didn't you arrest him?" she asks.

I chuckle, holstering my weapon. "Easy. I'm not a cop." Her gaze moves to my holster, alarm filling her expression, so I elaborate. "Private security." The half truth keeps me legitimate.

Her shoulders relax. "For the garage?"

"This hellhole? No. Just for you at the moment."

Her small smile is pure sunshine, and I want to nibble the area of her neck she just exposed by sliding her thick curls behind her ear.

"Now, about that dinner—"

"Look, it's not like I don't want to let James Bond take me out to dinner. Honestly, I'd love it. It's been a while since a man has bothered. But I might be in Chicago for a very short time. Maybe as short as one day."

She worries her lip between her teeth again. It's a tell. There's something she doesn't want to discuss. But it's not like I want to show her all the scars across my chest, abs, and heart, so maybe we're alike in that regard.

"How about this? No commitments. No phone numbers. Not even real names." Sure, I have access to hers, but that'll be my little secret.

"Why would you want that?"

"I need a night off," I tell her honestly. "I want to have a good time. Live a little. For the first time in a long time, spoil someone. Why not you?"

Shivering in her thin long-sleeve T-shirt, she considers it. I slip off my blazer and wrap it around her, giving her a minute to think it through . . . and giving me an excuse to stand so much closer.

"I—Irene," she says, bringing her fake name to the table.

Good. Now I need one.

I consider Magic Mike but opt for "Liam." I hold out a hand, formalizing our fake introductions. "First time in Chicago, Irene?"

Her nose crinkles, and it's absolutely adorable. "Is it obvious?"

I shrug with a grin. "North Carolina plates. Worst parking garage in the city."

"It's the closest place to the tower that took cash."

Tugging a twenty from her purse, she hands it over as if I just valeted her car. "Thank you."

It's an opportunity I take to wrap my hand around hers, smoothing my warmth over it. I love the feel of her soft skin, and after I've closed her hand tightly around her money, I keep holding on.

"Keep your cash. I'd prefer to show you Chicago. Spoil you like no one has. For one night only." I'm not really asking a question as much as making a small promise . . . to both of us.

I can't help but notice the condition of her car, along with a cute little stuffed animal that makes me wonder if "Irene" is younger than she looks. But she can't be that young.

"No strings attached?" she asks warily.

"No strings attached."

She bites her lower lip, and I can practically see the gears turn behind her brown eyes as she ponders my offer for a good long minute. "No strings? No commitments?"

"Scout's honor." I lift three fingers in a solemn vow. "Is that a yes?"

With the sweet curl of her full lips, I know she's decided before she even responds.

"Yes," she finally says.

"Keys," I say, holding out my hand and wiggling my fingers expectantly.

Confused, she cocks her head.

I walk past her and around to the passenger side of her car, a blue Civic that's seen better days. Opening the door she naively left unlocked, I don't give her any wiggle room to change her mind.

"If I drive, you'll get to see all the buildings you missed. I'm guessing you were too busy checking your GPS and maneuvering through the insane city traffic to enjoy it. It's your chance to relax and enjoy the ride."

CHAPTER 8
Ivy

"What's your favorite food?" Liam asks as he weaves in and out of traffic.

I crane my neck to take in one skyscraper after another as we make our way down the congested streets that he seems to know by heart. "Other than Carolina ribs with hushpuppies, I'm not really sure I have any."

It takes me a moment to realize that even when semi-suicidal tourists jump out in front of him like squirrels, Liam hasn't laid on the horn. Not once. It's hard not to compare him to Derrick, who's cocky. Brash. Impatient. Needy. Did I mention he sometimes cries after sex? Yup. One of those.

The man sitting beside me is the complete opposite of my exboyfriend. Calm. Collected. Hollywood good looks and in control. So in control, he held a gun to a man's chest and didn't raise his voice. My eyes wander down his suit as I wonder if he exerts control in every situation.

This is exactly the type of man I shouldn't want. Between the holster peeking from under his jacket to the trident tattoo at his neck, the man is the devil incarnate. Maybe it's the dry spell talking, but I want to sleep with Liam just to know how the other half lives. The mind-blowing-sex half.

But then he opens his mouth, and all bets are off. "What's a hushpuppy?"

A hand flies to my heart. "You did not just ask that."

He gives me a sideways glance. "Tell me it's not a puppy." His smile is just as dangerous as the rest of him. I have no doubt he knows exactly what he's doing when he flashes it. I'm not equipped to deal with a man like this.

I focus on his question. "It's a heavenly combination of cornmeal and spices that's deep-fried and served hot with honey butter."

He nods with approval. "You had me at honey butter." He flips his signal and cuts right. "Hopefully, this dinner is a close second."

When we roll to a stop before a valet station, my nerves get the best of me. I know this car might not look like much, but it's paid in full and constitutes the bulk of my worldly possessions.

Liam's hand covers mine, soothing me with a squeeze. "I know these guys, and they know me. Your car and everything in it are absolutely safe."

Breathing a little easier, I nod.

"Good evening, sir," a valet says, wearing a crisp white shirt and bow tie.

"Hey, John." Liam unfolds himself from my compact car and slips him what looks like two twenties before shaking his hand. "Take extra-special care of her."

Before I can object, another valet has opened my door wide. "Good evening, miss," he says, smiling as he waits for me to get out.

I try to, before realizing, like an idiot, that my seat belt is still on. I take a breath, unlatch myself, and accept Liam's expectant hand as he whisks me to the curb.

With two valets on standby and the kind of cash he's throwing around to take care of an eight-year-old economy car, my outfit isn't half good enough for tonight. Liam's wearing a blazer and slacks. I'm in a pair of jeans and a white long-sleeve T-shirt.

When Liam looks me up and down, my nerves flutter with uncertainty. His hand wraps around the small of my back, pulling my body next to his. "You're breathtaking, Irene."

It's at this point I realize I might be dreaming.

A slight blush warms my cheeks, but it's not because of what he says or how he says it. It's his piercing blue eyes. They sparkle when he says Irene, and the name isn't even mine.

"Thank you," I say softly, pretending I'm not half as self-conscious as I am.

He leads me inside, resting his hand so it barely touches the small of my back, but the heat melts me as we enter the restaurant. Rounded fish tanks form columns two stories high, and bronze letters line one wall, spelling HAYDON'S ON THE SHORE.

"The view of the water is a must-see, Irene."

"Wait." I plant my hand on his chest, momentarily struck by how built he is.

He saved my cash, then possibly saved my life. And after all that, and me giving him the incredible brush-off, he wants to take me to dinner at one of the most exclusive and expensive restaurants in Chicago. I know, because it's been on my top ten places to visit ever since it was featured on the Travel Channel.

"I can't let you do this."

"Have dinner with a beautiful woman?"

"Not when you look like that, and I look like this."

Liam sweeps me to a private corner of the entry. "You'd be more comfortable if we matched?"

"I'd feel more comfortable if you took me to a food truck. You've already done so much for me."

"Food truck, huh?"

The jaw he rubs has to have two days' worth of stubble, but it doesn't hide the dimple in his left cheek. The same way the sparkle in those bright blue eyes doesn't hide the pain behind them. Pain like I've seen in so many visitors at the center. Pain that can never be hidden because it comes from love.

Is that why he needs the freedom of no commitments?

"Out of the question. But . . ." Liam slides a hand up the wall, leaning closer to me. "I have a better idea. I'll be five minutes. Promise you won't go anywhere."

I swallow hard, and my words come out in a whisper. "I promise."

When he's gone, rushing back out the entrance, the minutes tick by way too slowly.

I'm underdressed, and I know it. Every time a woman walks by in six-inch heels and a cocktail dress that probably costs more than my car, I take another step back, trying and failing to blend into the woodwork.

It doesn't do any good.

One woman tries to hand me her cashmere coat. She's lucky I didn't keep it. Three different waitstaff ask if they can seat me or show me to the bar, but between their tone and the way they eye my outfit, all I can hear is *are you lost?* I don't belong here.

When the next person asks if I'm here to pick up Door Dash, I'm seconds from leaving. Liam said five minutes. It's been closer to fifteen, and I have no way to reach him. And no valet ticket to retrieve my car.

My eyes slam shut. *I'm an idiot.*

I race out the door, slamming into a man who grabs my arms and doesn't let me go.

"What's the rush?" he asks, and I almost don't recognize him.

Liam's light blue shirt is now more casual, sans tie, and the top two buttons are undone and paired with jeans that look tailor-made for him. His blazer and dress slacks are gone, along with the shoulder holster and gun, presumably tucked inside the shopping bag he's carrying.

Embarrassed and a little unprepared for the trouble he's gone to, I turn away. "You said five minutes."

His fingers lift my chin, and I see the unsettled tight line. "Sorry, I took a little longer than I thought."

I lower my voice. "I shouldn't be here."

"You're right," he says, stunning my mouth wide open. His arm wraps around me, and he turns me in the direction I came from. "You should be right over there." His electric blue eyes hold mine as I melt on the spot. "Don't go."

Don't go. Has a man ever asked me not to go? Suddenly, I'm not in the hurry I was to leave. His big hands are warm, making me feel safe.

"I am a little hungry," I admit. That makes his smile return, and mine as well. "Nice jeans."

"Now we match." Liam wings out an arm. "Ready?"

I've never had a man go to this much trouble—or any trouble —to make me feel comfortable. And I do. I'm so completely comfortable, I almost wish this was the start of something more.

I wrap my hands around a bicep carved of pure stone, reminding myself this is only for the night. That was my request as much as his.

As soon as we're seated, a tuxedoed sommelier holds up a bottle of wine in offering, displaying it to each of us. Before he begins describing the fine red, Liam interrupts him.

"No alcohol," he says easily, though he still checks with me. "Right?"

I love that he remembered that. Too impressed for words, I merely shake my head. But I don't want him not to drink just because I'm not. "Don't stop on my account. Haydon's is world-famous for their exquisite pairings."

"They are, but I actually don't drink either."

The sommelier nods, offering us an assortment of waters and sodas, as well as finely crafted virgin cocktails. I ask for the

Lavender Spritzer, while Liam opts for the hometown sophistication of a Coke with lime.

Our drinks arrive in minutes, and Liam proposes a toast. "To you. And a night neither of us will ever forget."

It's the perfect toast because, no matter what, it's already a night I'll never forget.

I clink my purplish-pink drink to his. "Cheers."

CHAPTER 9
Leo

After a sublime dinner of white truffle bucatini and butter-braised lobster tails, I'm still left wondering what held her so long outside D'Angelo Tower. But I'm too distracted by the sexy way she sucks her lip in between her teeth when she studies the dessert menu and can't decide. And because I can't decide between interrogating her or strip-searching her with my tongue, I summon the waiter.

"We'll have the caramel hazelnut crème brûlée and the chocolate praline mousse." She narrows her eyes. "There's an ancient proverb that says enlightenment comes with two desserts."

"I'll take all the enlightenment I can get."

Once the desserts are delivered with two incredibly tiny spoons, I scoop a small spoonful of chocolate mousse and hold it to her lips. "You were outside the building a long time."

Smiling, she takes a bite. *Mmm* vibrates from her lips before she speaks. "I stumbled upon an opportunity. It could change my life ..." she trails off.

"And that's a bad thing?"

She shrugs. "It might be."

She eagerly returns the favor, leaning in and feeding me a

spoonful of crème brûlée, and I can't help my own *mmm* as I savor the flavor.

We continue this ritual as I give her my two cents. A little advice I intend on following myself.

"Look, I don't know much about you or this opportunity. But I do know this. There are no second chances." I lean close to her neck. "Sometimes you have to throw caution to the wind."

"Throw caution to the wind," she repeats softly.

"Go after what you want." My teeth barely graze her ear as she snaps away.

Her eyes question mine for a long beat. There's enough heat blazing behind her eyes that I'm confident it'll shut down all the uncertainty that lingers there as well. But I don't push her. I sit back, sip the rest of my coke, and wait for her response.

"What if I don't know what I want?"

I kiss her fingertips. "Then I take you home."

The valet is there in no time, and we drive along in silence. I've lived in Chicago for a decade. The same gray buildings and overcast days. The same empty nights. I barely notice it as we drive along. But with Irene, it's all fresh and new. The city is one big twinkling adventure, not just a backdrop I could take or leave.

Maybe that's why I've latched on to her, soaking in her energy the way a tree reaches for the sun. I have a feeling that no matter how much of her I take in, it'll never be enough. And I haven't even slept with her. I almost feel bad that the evening is over.

Almost, until she asks, "Is the Bean around here?"

Is it? I get my bearings and cut a hard left, having decided that the evening is not over. She squeals with delight and grabs my hand. I lace my fingers in hers. *Definitely not over.*

Her stock value skyrockets when I suggest breaking into Millennium Park, and she doesn't bat an eye. It's midnight, and there's no better way to see the art of Chi-Town without another soul around. I usually escape here by myself, but when that angelic face asked about the Bean, how could I resist?

"It's huge."

Yup. You heard it here, folks. That's exactly what she said.

I glance up at the colossal sculpture I've seen a million times before, only now realizing that as many times as I've passed by it, this is the first time I've been here with anyone else. At all. The epiphany strikes me just as I realize she's absolutely right. It is huge.

"Three stories high and twice as long," she reads from her phone, enthusiasm popping from every word. "The Chicago Bean weighs a hundred ten tons. Roughly the weight of—"

"Fifteen elephants," I say in unison with Irene, having long ago memorized these facts. I gaze at her a little too long. Even in the low city lights, she's radiant.

"It's meant to look like liquid mercury." I step closer. "Cost twenty-three million dollars to construct." Another step. "And is filled to the brim with . . ." I'm close enough to skim my lips against her forehead, but I don't. "With Jelly Bellies."

She giggles. "Fifteen elephant tons of Jelly Bellies?"

"I was more wowed with the cost, but that's impressive, too."

Her body is front and center before mine. "Thank you for tonight, Liam." I have no idea what comes over me, but I don't kiss her. Or think about fucking her. The moment is too perfect. A cloudless night with a million twinkling stars and a soft breeze. Her big, dark eyes and something more than the smell of whatever perfume follows her wherever she goes. It's the scent of her, and it's intoxicating.

I pull out my phone, scrolling until I find the perfect background music. As Laura Fygi begins her rendition of "For Sentimental Reasons," I pocket my cell and sweep Irene's curves against my body, putting a month of dance lessons for my cousin's wedding to good use.

Her expression twists, suggesting she's confused and maybe

just a little on edge. "I thought you said no strings, Mr. Commitment-phobe?"

"This is not a commitment more than the one I proposed. Spoiling you."

Unconvinced by my objection, she clarifies her position. "I'm not looking for a relationship."

Her words are insistent, but her body relaxes, swaying with mine as if we've held each other this close for years, giving me every assurance that not only do I have her undivided attention but that she's damn good in bed.

"And I'm not asking for one. We've got several more hours before the sun comes up. I can still take you home ..."

"Or?" she asks, giggling.

"Or you stop staring at life from the sidelines. No holding back," I breathe against her temple. "Take what you want."

Her lips brush mine. "Take what you want, Liam." When she stresses the name of my alter ego, I'm hard as a rock. I have to kiss her. A real kiss. A first kiss that I can never take back. Considering it's been years since I've kissed a woman, she's lucky I don't swallow her whole.

I caress her cheek. I don't give a shit if this means more to me than it does to her, and I care even less that it means this much to me, but it does. So, I start slow and soft, inviting her instead of demanding because that can wait for later.

Her lips are shy when they part. A strange relief. When her mouth welcomes my tongue, I glide inside. Tasting. Exploring. Letting Liam know Irene differently than Leo would know a woman now. Shedding my armor to let her see the real me. A man I'm determined to button back up first thing in the morning.

Tonight, there are no expectations. No commitments. No consequences. And for Liam, no holding back.

We come up for air. "Fair warning." Her scowl is delectable, and her words are a siren's song. "I have a lot bottled up. Letting go might be explosive."

"I could use explosive," I say honestly, finding her eyes wide and engaging. "One night of anything less might not be enough."

"One night?" she whispers, needing reassurance.

I twirl her out, tug her back in, and swing her into a low dip. "One night." I lift her to her feet. "All mine until the sun rises."

She pulls away, and for a second, I can't read her.

It's a bad idea. A mistake. So, why am I pushing her into this? Why push myself? I take my own step back, pocketing my hands. "It's not too late. I can still take you home."

Her gentle fingers run along my scruff. She teases me with those full lips as she brushes them against mine. My tongue swipes hers for a second, and God, the woman still has the lingering taste of our second dessert. The indulgent chocolate is a heavenly swirl with her own flavor.

Denying it is pointless. I want her.

She enjoys a lingering kiss before whispering, "I'm ready to take what I want."

CHAPTER 10
Leo

"Jesus fucking Christ."

One foot inside the door of the hotel, and my pants are off, my shirt is off, and Irene is on her knees, letting me sink so far down her throat that I lose all shreds of control I have left. All I know is I have to thrust. And then the gorgeous goddess takes more.

"Fuck." I gasp, bracing against the wall for balance to keep myself from plowing into those sumptuous lips that are sucking me straight to oblivion.

How we made it to the hotel with our clothes intact is beyond me, but it's clear Irene has shed her shyness. And trust me, after my own dry spell, I. Am. Game. A hurried stop at a twenty-four-hour convenience store for condoms was agreed upon and absolutely required.

My fingers tighten in the soft curls of her hair, and I'm too tempted to keep the rhythm going because it's so good. She's so good. It takes every bit of my self-control to drag myself away from Irene's heaven of a mouth.

"Get on the bed," I order.

Her voice is breathless and choppy as she pants out, "Yes, sir."

I doubt she means to be as seductive and submissive as she is, but damn, I'm in so much trouble.

I don't have to ask her to strip off her bra and panties. The cream bra and soaked matching thong are on the floor in an instant, revealing so much soft toffee-colored skin that now I'm the one left panting and breathless.

"What's wrong?" she asks.

"Nothing," I say, letting my eyes linger. Nothing's wrong. Nothing except that this angel is about to be defiled in the most decadent ways, and I'm going to take my time undoing her.

Once both of us are stripped down to nothing but our tattoos and hungry gazes, she backs onto the mattress, spreading herself, and letting me see how wet she is. The sight of the fullness of her breasts, like the rest of her, draws me in until my tongue and lips make way for a soft tug with my teeth.

"Mmm."

Her moan hardens my cock to granite, making me wrap a fist around it and pump. It's still wet from her mouth, and I'm desperate, too ready to plow between her legs until I lose the lock on my self-control and our names all at once.

I tame my savage urges for a second, taking my time kissing and licking my way down her body, across the soft plane of her belly, along her thighs, and finally to her sweet, molten center.

Up to this point, her scent was laced with citrus and vanilla. But here, it's all her. An instant addiction I can deny all I want, but every cell in my body will crave it like oxygen long after tonight.

I take in a deep breath as the tip of my nose nuzzles the softness of her curled hair. Bare women are a dime a dozen, a female maintenance ritual I've never understood. This—the natural curls of an unstripped pussy—are a rare delicacy I want to indulge in.

Like a starved man, I devour her. I'm not gentle, and my stubble has to be rough, but she doesn't seem to mind. Irene moves like the ocean following the pressure of the wind, more responsive than any woman I've ever known. I don't back down. If anything, I demand more.

"Yes . . ." She sighs, arching her back and rocking her hips, so greedy with need.

When was the last time a man worshipped her?

She writhes against my mouth until I glide a long lick up her sweet folds and suck her budding clit. I'm barely a finger into her center when her body shudders and her walls clamp hard. So hard. And a stranger's name fills the air.

"*Liam!*"

I'm about to lose it, go absolutely ape-shit on the girl, until I realize that's me. She's screaming my name.

Yes, that's right, fuckers. In this moment, I am Liam. Let it echo through the walls for all the eleventh floor to hear as I take the first of many orgasms from the beautiful damsel known only as Irene.

Liam and Irene are so damn perfect together. A small part of me regrets that the blazing inferno between us won't last.

"Ready for more, angel?" I whisper as I nibble a spot on the inside of her thigh. I run my fingers down her belly, her darker skin a contrast to mine.

"More?" Her head flies up, and I can't believe she thinks I'd let her get away with one orgasm.

Is that what she's used to? A once-and-done? I mean, technically, we are a once-and-done, but not when it comes to the important things like desserts and orgasms.

Just when it comes to me. Does that make me an asshole?

"So much more," I say, kissing my way up her body as she runs her fingers through my hair.

Her legs ease around me, and I move into position, two puzzle pieces that inexplicably fit.

"Turn around," I demand, and the disappointment in her pout makes me kiss her. "What?"

"Nothing."

Her smile is forced, and she shifts slightly as if to obey, but she can't turn around. Not yet.

Resting more of my weight on her, I pin her in place. "Tell me."

I'm not sure I really want to hear about her disappointment that I'll be leaving in the morning. Wanting more than one night. Needing more than I can give. But with her breaths still trembling from the ecstasy I just gave her, and her dissatisfaction blaring, I have to know why.

As I nibble her neck, she finally confesses.

"It's just that I . . . I've never seen a man come. Never watched."

"Turn around."

"But I want to see you."

I place a kiss on her forehead, reassuring her. "You will."

When I sweep her body to the side, she rolls into the position I want. I have to get a better look at the ass that surpasses every ass I've ever seen.

I caress one tight, round cheek and then the other. For a woman who objected, Irene likes how I touch her, lifting her ass as if I'm molding her exactly where I want.

Fucking perfect. Not just her ass. *Her*. She's fucking perfect.

I almost wish it wouldn't end.

Gliding a condom onto my shaft, I'm so ready to plow into her that I pull in a breath, reassuring her. "I'm not going to come with you like this," I say as I inch in. "It's just one of a million ways I can think of to fuck your sweet pussy to oblivion."

Her pants rise to moans. "Then why the condom?" Impatient, my little Irene thrusts back.

Both my hands grip her hips, keeping her nice and still as I work another achingly slow inch into her tightness. And God, is she tight.

Why the condom? What she means to ask is why the condom right this second.

I don't have a good answer. Except after getting a front-row view of her from this angle, she's right. Whatever remaining control I possess is on a collision course with a climax that's been two years in the making.

Don't get me wrong. The shower has met my needs plenty. But trusting myself to pull out in time when I can feel the pulse of her walls against every inch of my dick? Not on your life.

I press light kisses to her back as I slide my hand around her, my fingers in position on her clit. Honest to a fault, I answer.

"Because I don't trust myself with you. As much as I'd like to think I'm a man of my word, I am still a man."

Her giggle subsides to a moan as she gives in to the light circles I move around her clit. "You definitely are."

Her body convulses hard and fast, and every part of my being is desperate to join her. Instead, I pull out, still rubbing slow waves of pleasure across her soaked pussy as I growl in her ear.

"Ready to watch, my little voyeur?"

"Yes."

"Work for it, angel. But I promise you, I'm not done."

Before she can ask, I'm on my back, lifting her into a straddle on top of me. She moves herself along the length of my shaft, knowing not only what I need, but what she needs as well.

Even if I had her every hour of every day, it wouldn't be enough. Thank God I'm going cold turkey after this. A distraction like the mysterious Irene isn't exactly conducive to compartmentalizing my life.

She isn't sentimental when my hand cups her cheek. Her full lips suck in my thumb as she rocks her way down my dick and fucks me like the Kentucky Derby's at stake. I'm burning up, a meteor seconds from colliding into her before the explosion is ripped from my body, taking another one from her in the process.

Exhausted, she collapses onto the hundred million shards of me still heaving in her wake. I wrap my arms around her sweat-drenched body as our heavy breaths float us back to earth. Eagerly, my fingers travel across her skin, memorizing every shape and curve. Giving me enough to fuel my fantasies for months—maybe years—to come.

As soon as I skim the tempting arc on the underside of her butt, my cock twitches. Her fingers wrap around it in an instant.

"So soon?" she asks.

I don't know what's gotten into me.

Scrap that. I know exactly what's gotten into me. Her.

"I said I wasn't done. And a promise is a promise."

I'm not sure when we got to sleep. Minutes ago. Hours? But at a quarter past five, I decide that even though I'll be doing the walk of shame out of here, the heavy aroma of sweat and sex means a shower is in order before I leave.

Being quiet, I step into the shower, trying to wash away all traces of a woman whose touch still burns along every square inch of my skin. Even in the strong scented lather of the hotel soap, she's everywhere, in all those places I don't need her to be right now. My thoughts. My heart? Clouding my brain with random thoughts like, does she like coffee in the morning? How does she take it? Sugar? And cream?

My gut tells me that if we did share a cup, she'd want it black. Extra strong. And not waste too much time savoring it because she's always on the go.

Like I am.

My heart squeezes.

I remember the last time I made coffee for a woman, which is why coffee is a bad idea. Completely out of the question. And if she stayed for coffee, coffee would lead to kissing, and kissing would lead to sex, and sex would mean feeding an addiction that won't be satiated until at least three o'clock in the afternoon. Leaving my boss no choice but to fire me because when confronted with the needs of my profession and the needs of my dick, is it even a choice?

Another one of a million reasons to go cold turkey.

My cock isn't listening. It lengthens, thick with need, which just reaffirms what I've said all along. Any excuse to stick around is a bad, bad, bad idea. Coffee is off the table. Sinking my fingers, tongue, or dick back into any part of her is off the table.

But no matter how much I try to convince myself, once I walk out of this bathroom and see her toned thighs and edible curves wrapped in soft hotel sheets, I'm not entirely sure my brain will override my cock. Only one way to know for sure.

Without bothering to dry off, I wrap a plush towel loosely around my hips and open the door. Even if she passes on coffee or breakfast or even me, there's no way that sexy little vixen is going anywhere without giving me the one thing I have to have.

Her name.

Her *real* name. Of her own volition so I can give her mine, two people meeting and knowing each other in this version of reality.

I don't want her remembering this night with Liam. I want her to know me as Leo. And as much as it pierces my heart with an ice pick when I think of it, the truth is, I want more.

I step out of the bathroom, and even in the dark, I can tell no one's in the bed.

"Irene?"

A quick glance around the suite reveals it's as empty as this bedroom. I flip on the lights and scan the nightstands, table, and desk. No note. In a few rushed steps, I'm at the window and catch a glimpse of her little blue compact car zipping away.

Maybe it's for the best. She said she didn't want a commitment. At least, not when the night began.

My eyes narrow on the car in the distance. There's no way I can see her license plate from here, not that I need it.

The small chime on my phone reminds me that I've got a little time to grab a cup of coffee. I check out the complimentary toiletries on the bathroom counter and make my early morning decisions. Teeth brushing in. Shaving out. Plus, I didn't exactly pack for the occasion, so I'll be parading my morning-after look through a long day of interviews.

But come early evening, the hunt begins. Judith owes me some paperwork.

Knock-knock-knock.

My heart leaps—actually skips a beat—when I hear someone knocking at the door. Maybe she came back and wants more. Coffee. Breakfast. Dinner. My name.

Play it cool. Maybe she just left something behind.

Still in the towel, I open the door, disappointed to see a bellman there. He nods at me. Certain the man standing before me has seen much worse, I don't even flinch. He hands me a shopping bag, the one I'd left in the trunk of her car last night and had completely forgotten about.

"Just a moment," I say, fishing a twenty from my wallet and handing it to him before shutting the door.

I know what's inside the bag, but I set it on the bed to check. Inside is my blazer, slacks, tie, holster, gun, and a note. A small sheet of paper from the hotel notepad.

You're an amazing man.
Thank you for sharing this part of yourself.
It's a night I'll never forget.

After rereading the three short lines a few more times, I realize this will be as close to happily-ever-after as I should venture to go. She deserves a man who will choose her. Every goddamned time. Always her.

I was right to go with my gut. I have a job to do. People to protect. A promise to a dying man I intend to keep.

It's a night I'll never forget, too. But it's time to say goodbye.

CHAPTER 11
Leo

"Y ou're late," Smoke says, frowning at me as I step into the kitchen and help myself to a cup of black coffee.

Not that I need it. I'm still wired from last night, but as far as Smoke is concerned, the less he knows, the better. "I'm five minutes early."

Smoke passes me a list of what I assume are the candidates we're interviewing today for the caregiver position. Fifteen women and three men. "I thought math was your strong suit." I smirk.

"Last minute add-on. Which means the fun starts that much sooner."

I stifle a yawn and take another look. "Men?" I give him an incredulous look. "Why the hell would we want men?"

"The attorneys insist that unless I want to get my ass sued for discrimination, taking the interview is the easier path."

"I'm no lawyer," I say, as if Smoke doesn't know, "but isn't this the equivalent of getting maimed by a lion and being forced to pet a few just to get acclimated? No matter how domesticated they may seem, they'll always be the enemy. Not to mention it'll probably trigger some seriously fucked-up PTSD."

As footsteps approach, we both zip it. We both know her footsteps by heart. Light. Timid. And seconds from entering.

Trinity D'Angelo. The crimes against her were enough to transform Smoke into the man he is today. Angry at the world and hungry for blood.

"Morning, Trini," Smoke says, sweeping his sister into an embrace she eases into. When she doesn't hug him back, it doesn't break his heart the way it used to. Instead, it fuels his fury.

In all the years I've wished her a good morning, she merely gives me a polite nod. Her mouth doesn't always lift to a smile, though it tries, but she never speaks. Still, there's a small amount of hope inside me, the tiniest glimmer that one day, she will.

"Good morning." After waiting a beat, I return the coffee to my lips for a sip.

Her thick blonde hair, still damp from the shower, clings to her cheeks, and her sweatshirt is the one she wore the first day we met. From the outside, she looks the same. But she's not that girl anymore.

Confident and competitive, Trinity was in her second year of college back then, when the biggest thing on her mind was beating her brother's MCAT scores. Back when Antonio D'Angelo ran the estate. When I was the outsider that he always treated like another son.

Smoke has her coffee ready, handing it to her as a store-bought muffin grabs her interest. She prefers the routine of a banana muffin, so we keep them stocked. It's then that I see the bandage peeking out from beneath her sleeve.

With a small book in hand, she heads out to the west lawn. To read, maybe, or to write. I can't tell if the book she's holding is a journal, but whatever it is, I hope it gets her closer to freedom from the nightmares and pain that plague her.

"Where were we?" Smoke asks as soon as she's out of the room.

"Some stranger watching over Trinity. Bad idea, interviewing men for the job. Worst fucking idea I've ever heard."

"Don't hold back," Smoke says before tearing into a piece of toast. By his tightly clenched jaw, it's obvious I'm preaching to the choir. "If we make a selection before the men are interviewed, which I've scheduled for last, then we don't have to interview them. It's that simple."

His attention shifts out the window as I polish off the last of my coffee and stew over it.

"So, not only are we making a selection today, we need to make it in the first fourteen candidates."

"Pre-selection. Contingent on a drug screen and background check." Squinting, Smoke focuses on something in the distance.

When he waves me over, I take a look and freeze. Normally I'd be ready to let my team know there's something they need to check out, but not this.

"What the hell?" Grappling at my composure, I try to temper the alarm in my voice. When Smoke shoots a glance at me, I know I've failed.

"Friend of yours?" he asks, but I'm too stunned to respond. "Is she changing her clothes? In her car?"

When Smoke has the audacity to add, "Let me get my binoculars," I growl. Actually growl at the man who could quash my career like a grape. As he chuckles at me, I fume.

For a girl adamant about not being committed, she certainly managed to hunt me down fast. Sure, I might have her name and her license plate number, but it's not like I showed up at her office. Or stripped in front of her boss. Not that we can see any of her goods, but the smartass grin beaming from Smoke's face has me clenching my fists to avoid any attempt at punching him.

Heated, I stalk to the door. "I'll find out what's going on."

Smoke chuckles. "Not calling the team to check it out?"

Fuck. I need to keep my cool. That son of a bitch will have eyes on us the whole time. Probably from all three angles of the cameras. With the audio jacked up, no doubt, because that's what I would do.

A small tinge of fear courses through me.

What did her note say? *Thank you for sharing this part of yourself.*

I used a condom. I mean, the first two times, for sure. How long does it take to get the results from a pregnancy test? Was that the reason she rushed out the door? That whole women's intuition deal? That is a thing, right?

My vision tunnels and my heart pounds so hard, it's the only thing I can hear.

Sure, I've thought about how life has dealt me a raw deal, and that I would have been a good dad. Goddammit, I would have been a great dad. But I don't even know this woman. So, why do a dozen baby names flip through my head? With the soft espresso tones of her skin, and my blue eyes that never peg me as Italian, what would our child look like?

Or what if she thought I was a D'Angelo? Every one of the D'Angelo men have an inherent distrust of women, and it wouldn't be the first time a woman has tried to impregnate her way into matrimony. I let my guard down, and I shouldn't have. What if she thought I was a D'Angelo?

Fuck. I fell for her.

But can anyone blame me? She's got the smile of an angel, the body of Jessica Rabbit, and in case those in the back missed it, her taste is goddamned addictive.

This is not my fault.

Irene—or Olivia, or whatever the hell her name is—is an addiction, and addictions need treatment. Cold turkey. No rubbing my cheeks over her silky-smooth thighs. No swirl of citrus and vanilla. No lapping up every last ounce of nectar until I'm dizzy with delighting her. And as I keep reminding myself with every step I take toward her as I watch her slip her clothes back on, no rock-hard boners.

If my dick would take the hint, that would be great.

Well, the joke's on you, sweetheart. I'm not a D'Angelo, and I never will be.

But . . . *shit*. Just because I'm not a real D'Angelo doesn't mean she isn't really pregnant.

My strides turn into stomps, getting louder and louder the closer I get, and I remind myself to play it cool.

But the second our eyes meet, we both say the same thing in unison.

"What the fuck?"

CHAPTER 12

Ivy

I f I thought of sneaking into Aunt Grace's house undetected before the crack of dawn, the woman sets me straight. I barely have a key in the door when she pulls it wide open. "Caught ya," she teases.

Nothing and no one ever got by Aunt Grace. Hence her becoming the cool aunt. With the aroma of coffee and apple muffins thick in the air, I know the drill. Food for details. Well, she's about to get an earful, whether she's ready or not. "Tell me you were out all night doing something exciting. Like dancing in a music video."

Her hair still in large foam rollers, her pink velour tracksuit makes me smile. "You should be in a music video."

"You haven't seen the best of it." She whips around so I can see J-U-I-C-Y across her backside, gives it a shake, and spins back around. "Come on. Tell me everything."

I tell her a few innocent details of my encounter with the smoking hot rebound god Brooke conjured, leaving it at, "He was nice."

She grabs my hand, lifting my palm to my face. "Maybe he's the one."

74

"There's only one man I'm interested in. Remember the photo?"

Aunt Grace nods as she tops off my coffee. "You found out who he is."

"Maybe. I was filling out a job application, making small talk with the woman at the front desk, Judith, and she remarked how much I looked like—" The name *Antonio D'Angelo* is on the tip of my tongue, but for some reason, I can't say it. The thought of some rich and powerful man being my father chokes me. Because it can't be true, can it?

And what if it is true? That means my father abandoned me. Hope and fear, excitement and rage all blur together, and I have no idea what I'm supposed to feel.

"Like who, hunny?" she asks, pulling a pill from a pharmacy container and breaking the little dot in half.

"Like ... someone in the building." Curious, I read the instructions. "This says *take one pill with food*. Not half a pill."

She waves me off. "This makes them last longer."

Am I the only one that makes no sense to?

She swallows it back and nudges me to continue.

I secretly snap a shot of her medication and look it up as I keep talking. "I'm going to research him a little today. Maybe try to catch up with him."

Used to treat blood pressure.

Before I can tear into her about the dangers of shorting her medication, my cell rings. UNKNOWN flashes across the screen. Along with the time. Barely six in the morning. Did Liam track me down?

I hold the phone tight to my ear as Aunt Grace keeps her big eyes fixed on mine. "Is it him?" she whispers.

I shush her with a finger to my lips. I feel a goofy smile forming. "Hello?" I answer in a sultry voice that came out of nowhere.

"Is this Olivia Palmer?" a woman asks.

"Yes."

"Hi, it's Judith. We met yesterday. I was looking at your application, and you might be a terrific candidate, but the only interview slot I have left is the first one of the day. Eight-thirty."

"Today?" I check my watch. That doesn't give me much time.

"Yes, dear. They're only doing interviews today, and it's the only slot. Can you make it?"

Relieved that I might not have to go crawling back to Derrick for a job or leave town when I'm so close to finding my father, I agree. "Yes. I can make eight-thirty." By the skin of my teeth with that God-awful parking. "At the Tower?"

"No. I can text you the address. You'll be interviewed on-site. Good luck."

Stunned, I have a million questions, but before I can ask any of them, Judith hangs up. I barely have time to brush my teeth. Rushed, I head to the suitcase I never got around to unpacking and scramble to find the blazer and dress Brooke loaned me.

"Can I help?" Aunt Grace sweetly asks, intuitive as she brushes my hair.

I hand her my cell and open the text. "Can you punch the address into Google?"

"I'm on it." A second later, she waves my phone at me. "Found it. It looks like some sort of compound. With a moat."

"What?" I look at the aerial view. It's large. Much bigger than Sparrow's facility, at least from what I can tell. Some of the property seems to be blurred out. From what I can see, it's surrounded by gardens and water features, and I can't wait to check out the inside. "It's beautiful."

"It's nearly an hour away," she insists, with her hands to my back. "Let me know how it goes."

"I will," I promise.

The guard checks the front and back of my driver's license. He makes a quick call while I confirm this is 7284 Keeton Road.

He nods, expressionless. "Yes."

I notice a plaque lodged into the guardhouse. The same letter D. And below it, the words, "D'Angelo Estate."

D'Angelo? As in D'Angelo Tower? And Antonio D'Angelo? The man who might be my father might be here? I might meet him. I bite my lower lip, on the verge of hyperventilating when the guard returns.

"Sorry, they didn't have you on the roster. I had to call head-quarters to confirm you're cleared for the job."

"The job?" I say, stunned. Realizing that people can just roll up to the property like it's a national park and that he might shoot me, I nod. "Yes. I'm here for the job."

Something I imagine is a smile passes his lips as he hands back my driver's license and gives me the okay to proceed.

"Follow the path to the front of the house. Pass the round-about, and park along the side. Another guard will meet you at the door. If you wander off on your way between your car and the door, you'll be trespassing. We don't take kindly to trespassers."

The intimidating guard places a hand on his holstered weapon, a gesture that's meant to be a warning. Instead, it reminds me of Liam.

My upbringing forces me to smile and thank the guard because no matter how unsettled we Southerners are, we're always ready with hospitality and a smile. If we were back home, after an intro like that, a fresh-baked biscuit and a tall glass of iced tea wouldn't be out of the question.

Nervous, I nod, then drive slowly past a thicket of trees to what appears to be the White House. *I can do it. Exactly what Liam said. Take what I want. Show him the photo, tell him who I am, and ask him about a million questions. If he doesn't throw me out on my ass...*

A very well-dressed woman is leaving as I pull up. In her smart suit and elegant hair styled in a sleek bun, she heads toward a Lexus convertible, a car that seems just right for a place like this. She's exactly what people here would look like. Polished. Professional. And not too happy, because God forbid, people crack a smile in these parts.

The longer I look at her, the harder I bite my lip. They have gates. They have guards. They have gardens and a water feature that looks like a fucking moat. What the hell am I doing here?

I swallow hard. *Think.* I need a strategy. Oh, I know. *Knock-knock. It's your daughter. Show me my room, then let's catch up on the last twenty-four years.* I'm pretty sure every guard around here is just itching for target practice.

I make myself busy, messing with my phone as I wait for her to leave because the last thing I need is an audience. Stripping in a car in broad daylight isn't ideal, but desperate times and all that. Once she pulls away, I see the letters on her door. *Stella's Bakery.* A shy glance at the mansion makes me realize it's twice the size of the assisted living center, and catering to the people inside must be more than a job for one person.

With a once-over of my clothes from last night and the just-sexed smell all over me, I grab the smart black blazer Brooke loaned me and a pretty pink dress that has enough stretch that I can pull it over my head. In this outfit, I'll be dressed almost as good as the caterer. The wrinkles aren't horrible. Squinting, I blur my vision, still seeing long creases across the clothes. *I really should've unpacked.*

I tuck Mr. Whiskers into a pocket of the blazer and swallow the feelings that try to surface every time I think of Liam. And I can't stop thinking of him.

With a touch of lip gloss, I smile at my reflection in the visor's mirror, transforming into a woman well suited to step up to the D'Angelo estate.

Before I replace the visor, I blink hard, realizing he's right there.

Liam from last night. And this morning.

Liam, who's moving way too fast toward my car.

Liam, who unraveled every thread holding me together, shattered me into a million pieces, and left me with nothing but two torturous words.

No commitments.

What's he doing here? Did he change his mind? Is he chasing me down? But . . . did he come from the front door? Does he live here?

Stepping out of the car, I come face to face with a dream man who might just be my worst nightmare.

We say it at the same time. "What the fuck?"

Alarmed, Liam unbuttons his blazer, pockets his hands, and steps into my space. "What are you doing here?"

Don't panic. Inhale in. Exhale out.

My eyes lock on to his. It can't be what I think it is. Just a crazy misunderstanding that we'll all laugh about.

I struggle to dislodge a lump of incomprehensible dread. "Liam? You . . . live here?"

His hard stare is unnerving. "Are you hoping I live here?"

Oh. My. God. Oh-my-God, oh-my-God, oh-my-GOD!

Shit, the D'Angelos live in Chicago. Antonio D'Angelo probably has lots of children. But I never, ever, *ever* imagined . . .

Liam looks over his shoulder before leaning in. In that low, raspy tone that had me spreading my legs a few hours ago but now is giving me the heebie-jeebies, he says, "What happened to no commitments?"

I have no idea what he's saying, but his mouth is moving, so he must be saying something. All I know is I'm about to hurl. The thought of accidentally screwing your brother can do that to a person.

"I'm going to be sick."

"Sick?" His eyes wide, he lifts both palms in surrender before raking his hands through his hair. "Stay calm," he says firmly. "You need to breathe. We both need to breathe."

Is he hyperventilating? Does he know I'm his sister?

Taking in short, choppy breaths, he stares me square in the eyes. "Who-who-who. Hee-hee-hee."

Is he doing Lamaze?

Mortified, I slam my eyes shut. My best bet is to get my ass back in the car, head home at about a hundred eighty miles per hour, step into a scalding-hot shower for three days straight, and put this whole ungodly mess behind me.

For the first time in my life, I believe that Mama was right. I should have never, ever, *ever* tried to track down my father. What the hell was I thinking?

"This was a mistake. I have to go," I say, determined to head back to North Carolina and take a Plan B pill. Just in case.

Liam opens his mouth, but it's someone else who speaks.

"Go?" a deep, resonating voice asks from behind me.

I whirl around.

The commanding man standing there is all muscles and tattoos and scowl, but his expression softens in an instant. "Are you Ms. Palmer?"

Meekly, I nod. "Y-y-yes."

He holds out a large hand, which swallows mine when I extend it for a shake. "Smoke."

"No, thank you." I wave off the offer. Not only because I don't smoke, but just the thought of it compounds my guilt and queasiness. As it is, it's all I can do to keep from upchucking all over the nice man's shoes.

Amused, he chuckles. "That's my name. My actual name is Mason D'Angelo, but I go by Smoke. And if you're nervous about the interview, don't be. We don't bite."

With the marks that prove otherwise, I say a silent prayer that none of them are visible. Heat sears up my neck and face as Liam and I glance at each other. Hiding my emotions has never been my forte, and guilt is the worst.

Smoke releases my hand and gestures toward the house. "After you," he says, not giving me the option to back away.

After an awkward moment, I glance longingly at my car before I take a few deliberate steps toward the house, followed closely by the two men.

If I wanted to get to know my father, now's my chance. Nothing makes a good impression with your long-lost dad like fucking your brother. I don't need an interview—I need a church. Although I'm not Catholic, confession sounds really, really good right now.

Once inside, Smoke leads us back to an office, a room with fine-finished wood shelves lining every wall, a stone fireplace taller than me, and an entire wall of floor-to-ceiling windows that overlook lush gardens. The two men pause at a set of wingback chairs, but don't sit until I do on the long leather sofa across from them.

I notice a small bar, and though I avoid alcohol like married men, I'd take a glass of just about anything right now.

Smoke passes a sheet of paper to Liam. It looks like my application.

"And you are Olivia," Liam says.

I'm not sure why he's saying it like that—like an accusation. He had an alias last night just like I did. And if anyone has a right to be mad, it's me.

Sure, we agreed on no real names. But how was I supposed to know who he was? As a matter of fact, this *is* my first rodeo. Next time I decide to have sex with someone, I'll insist on a pre-test with 23andMe.

It isn't until both of them are staring at me that I realize I've pulled Mr. Whiskers from my pocket and am petting him to within an inch of his life. Instantly, I stop. Mortified, I release a nervous giggle and hold him high for both to see.

"This is Mr. Whiskers. Mr. Whiskers and the use of small stuffed animals, is one of many therapies I explore early on with a new client because he's small and nonthreatening. It can help ground someone to a place and time when they felt safe. Each person is unique. How they respond to something as innocent as a stuffed animal gives clues to what might speak to them on a greater scale, especially with people who are timid or nonverbal. Is the person you look after nonverbal?"

"She has been for the most part," Smoke says, answering with gentle eyes and a smile that relaxes me.

Liam speaks, still seething. "Since we're all doing introductions, including Mr. Whiskers, I'm Leo."

"Yes," Smoke says, much less irritated. "Leo Zamparelli, my chief of security."

What did he say?

"Zamparelli," I say, repeating his last name a little too loudly. "Not D'Angelo."

"No." It's Leo who answers, and the confirmation fills me with relief.

Thank the Lord. He's not my brother. My shoulders drop, and both my hands land on my chest. Finally, I can breathe again.

Until Leo says, "Disappointed?"

His tone is harsh. It's probably not helpful that while he seems closed off and cold, I release a loud sigh and a giggle. Reconsidering my erratic behavior, I blow out a long breath, intent on regaining my composure. I am, after all, in the middle of an interview.

"No." I clear my throat. "Not at all."

Leo tilts his head, and his eyes narrow. "Are you sure that's not a problem, Ms. Palmer?"

Problem? Definitely not. Trust me, the last thing I need on my résumé is *brother lover.*

It takes me a beat to realize he's irritated. When I do, I straighten in my seat. "No. I . . . it's a long story."

"I'll bet it is." The blast of arctic chill that comes from him isn't exactly subtle. He follows it with, "I'm sorry, I'm not sure the job is what you're looking for."

What? I blink, questioning him with my eyes. I can't believe he would try to block my interview. Should I bring up Sin? Or the photo?

Stay calm.

"But it is," I say stubbornly. "And I assure you, my references are impeccable. I've assisted people in varied medical and cognitive conditions. And of all ages. Could you tell me more about the person I would be assisting?"

Obviously noticing the glances passing between Leo and me, and a slew of invisible messages even I don't know how to interpret, Smoke says, "The candidate we select would be assisting a woman, twenty-five years old. She suffered through a trauma four years ago."

Her age shocks me. She's only a year older than me.

"Traumatic injury?" I ask. It would make sense if she played sports in college.

He nods so solemnly, I know there's more. "Emotional trauma as well."

The woman he's talking about might be a stranger, but it's also possible that she's my sister. My only sister. I'm more determined than ever to be here for her. To help in any way I can.

"Well, we have a lot of candidates to interview," Leo says abruptly. "Thank you for your time."

If Leo thinks he can just send me on my way because he's a little uncomfortable about us sleeping together, he'd better think again.

I don't hold back, shedding all that wholesome humility in favor of flaunting my skills. "I've also been doing research on music therapy for victims of post-traumatic stress disorder. It's in partnership with several veterans in my local area."

Leo scoffs. "I'll just bet it is, Olivia."

I don't even know what the hell Leo is driving at, but in the bright light of day, the artist formerly known as Liam is the world's biggest ass.

I pull in a breath to calm myself. "Actually, I go by Ivy."

Frowning, Smoke rises to his feet. "Leo, can I speak to you in the hall?"

Even with his new name hovering between us, this is Liam, isn't it? Same rich blue eyes and intense stare. Same shirt he was wearing last night, though a little more rumpled today. If I peeled that sexy shirt away, he'd have the same tattoos across his chest and abs.

So, why doesn't he act like Liam? Or is Liam a lie as much as his name? Just a façade, a perfect candy-coated shell of a man named Leo?

As Smoke and Leo file out of the room, I step over to the elegant set of French doors and contemplate my next move. I can't leave without at least meeting my father. See his face and let him see mine.

A woman walks across the grounds, and I wonder if that's her. My sister. Even from this far away, her age seems right. The sunlight halos her flowy blonde hair, carrying her through her walk with the brightness of an angel and the heaviness of a ghost, and all I can do is wonder.

What happened to her?

CHAPTER 13
Leo

"Something you wanna tell me, Mr. *Not-D'Angelo*? Like why you got all throat-punch possessive when I saw her changing. Or why, despite the obvious fact that there's something going on between the two of you, you seem to have no idea what her name is."

After I make a few stops and starts, letting my mouth open and close with nothing coming out but a weak gasp of air, Smoke crosses his arms. By the look on his face, he isn't sure if the answer will annoy him or amuse him.

I'm pretty sure both. Especially with the shit grenade I'm about to toss at him. "Remember the girl I was speaking to yesterday?"

His eyes widen with amusement as he slaps my shoulder briskly. "So much for one date," he chuckles. "And why didn't you know her name?"

I blink. Without a good way to say *I seduced a woman incognito*, I screw up my face, trying to find an answer. Instead, I duck and avoid. "In what universe is Ivy short for Olivia?"

"Ivy is actually short for Olivia or Vivian," Smoke says, and when I shoot him a sideways glance, he's ready with a response before I have to ask the question. "It was one of the considerations for Trinity's name. Before my brothers saw *The Matrix* and banded together to outvote the rest of us. Only three of us were actually named by Mom and Dad. So, back to you and Ivy. You have a . . . connection?"

If you call being balls-deep in that goddess's body a connection, then sure.

Shrugging, I nod.

Smoke narrows his gaze on me. "I'm not going to ask about your private life because *A*, I don't need to know. And *B*, I don't want to know."

Still, I feel compelled to explain. To say something about the smallest possibility that this woman could be pregnant with my child. And since Smoke's technically a doctor, he could advise me. Or kill me. He tends to be unpredictable that way.

Before I can get half a word out, Smoke lifts his palm toward my face, indicating I shouldn't bother. "Bottom line? Fix it, Leo. On paper, she's the best candidate we have. Usual background check. Find out who she is. If she's clean, we hire her. And if she's not . . ."

We both know how that sentence ends because it usually ends with me.

This is exactly the reason I don't do relationships. But for Christ's sake, can't a guy have a one-night stand without a landfill of regret?

"I need to make a call," Smoke says with a sigh. "Get rid of her for today. We'll keep interviewing candidates."

I nod. Once he's out of the room, I tuck her résumé in my pocket and head back to his office, summoning all the strength I need to be alone in a room with her.

And not have my way with her on the middle of my boss's desk.

CHAPTER 14

Leo

Of course, since Smoke and I are in his private residence, it was oh-so-wise of us to leave Ivy completely alone. In Smoke's private office. From which, of course, she is now missing.

"Shit." *Can this day get any fucking worse?*

Sucking in a long breath through my nose, I let out my frustration and reach for my phone, ready to tap into the security cameras that cover the estate's twenty-some rooms, twelve baths, hallways, kitchen, foyer, and forty square acres of land. The feeds come up, but I don't need them. It only takes a second to realize the back door is cracked open.

As soon as I step outside, I see them. In the distance is Ivy, dangerously close to Trinity. Watching Ivy wade in the knee-high water is confusing. But when she pulls Trinity in, shoes and all, confusion gives way to outright panic.

I've spent too many hours of the last four years protecting her. The thought of failing now turns my blood to ice. Feet pounding and Glock drawn, there's no room for rational thought. I'm at the mercy of a decade of military training and the vow I made to Antonio D'Angelo.

Weapon in hand, I approach. "Step away from her."

Panic flashes across Ivy's expression, and for a second, all I see is her face last night.

Across from me. Under me. Filled with me. And fuck, I freeze.

In the next second, Trinity steps between the two of us, knee-deep in the small pond. Instantly, I lower my weapon, prepared to destroy any progress Trinity and I have made over the past four years by yanking her out to keep her safe. Instead, she steps forward, leading with a soft smile.

"It's all right, Leo," she says, holding a baby swan high in her hands. And I'm at a loss.

Did Trinity speak to me?

Stunned, I'm struggling to form a coherent sentence as Ivy helps her out of the water.

"You can put it away," she says so softly, my only response is to comply. So, I do, holstering my weapon as I stare at her in absolute disbelief.

Sure, I've heard her speak, but only with the limited number of words required. And never, not once, has she spoken to me. Not since before the attack, which has been a lifetime of wondering if she would ever be all right. She sounds all right, and the relief that fills me chokes me up. A telltale prickle starts behind my eyes.

Heavy footsteps approach. *Smoke.*

The single sniffle that comes from me is completely unexpected. "Allergies," I blurt before clearing my throat.

Smoke steps up to me, assessing me because there's a full-grown man a millisecond from openly weeping on his lawn. His scrutinizing glance passes to each of us, finally landing on Trinity. "Trini? Everything all right?"

She wraps an arm tight against her brother while cooing at the little swan. "We rescued her." Just like with me, as soon as she speaks, her small act of normalcy shakes him. He hugs her back, hard, and kisses the top of her head.

"I'm so glad that Ivy will be here," Trinity says softly.

His head swings up, and the weight of his heated glare lands squarely on me. I shrug as innocently as I can, a move that makes the angry vein in his forehead bulge to a point that it's seconds from bursting.

Just as she did by stepping between me and Ivy, Trinity protects me, her slim fingers smoothing Smoke's cheek. "Hey. Leo had nothing to do with this. I figured if you're picking out an assistant for me, I'd have the final say. And I choose Ivy."

Under his breath, Smoke speaks with pain in his words. "I can't promise that yet."

"Why not?" Trinity asks simply as if she's merely rebuffing an argument for Chinese takeout.

"Yes," Ivy says, suddenly confident and ballsy. She even has the audacity to cross her arms stubbornly over her chest. Which I'm now staring at. "Why not?"

I should be doing my job, separating the D'Angelos from a woman whose charms seem to be working on everyone around her. Even me.

Smoke looks at me, and I look at him, because what can we do? The two women pit themselves together against us, and they're freaking adorable.

I shake off Ivy's powerful voodoo spell. "We're not making any decisions immediately," I say, hoping to defuse whatever the hell's going on and get Ivy off the property. At least for today. "We still have a long list of candidates to interview, and it's in everyone's best interest to see the process through."

"But—" Trinity's objection barely hits the air before Ivy interrupts her.

"It's all right." Ivy strokes Trinity's arm, and they exchange a glance that doesn't make sense. Like two people who've known each other a lot longer than a few minutes at most, sending and receiving secret pieces of code. "Mr. Zamparelli is right. You have my contact information. I'll see myself out."

"That's not how this works, Ms. Palmer," I say firmly. "I'll escort you out."

But before Ivy can step away, Trinity pulls her into a hug so tight, I'm not entirely positive she intends to let her go. It's apparent Smoke and I have missed something important and big, and it's also apparent that whatever it was is staying between the two of them.

Ivy's whisper isn't low enough to prevent us from hearing. "It's okay. They're just looking out for you."

Exactly. Thank you. Even Ivy—a woman who's one big avalanche of suspicious activity—clearly sees that everything we do is for Trinity's own good.

Eventually, Trinity lets go, leaving me to deal with Ivy's cold shoulder.

Frowning, Ivy brushes past me, and I don't blame her. Pulling a gun on her first thing the morning after wasn't exactly the best way to score points, but at least now she knows exactly where I stand on everything.

I vowed long ago that I'd protect the D'Angelos with my last fucking breath, and I will. Even from her.

CHAPTER 15

Leo

"I don't need an escort. I know my way out," Ivy says. Her body is tense and angry, a tightly wound tornado ready to tear me limb from limb.

But no matter how rushed her steps are or how quickly she marches away, I'll be exactly eighteen inches from her at all times. Which is the established proximity for escorting a person off the property when they don't require restraints.

Trust me, no one is more disappointed than I am that restraints won't be making an appearance.

"This isn't about what you need," I say, explaining with a matter-of-fact and professional demeanor. Under my breath, I add, "Unlike last night," letting all that noble professionalism fly right out the fucking window.

I needed to get that small tantrum out of my system. Because in case she didn't get the memo, I'm pissed. And maybe she's the mother of my child because that's the kind of day I'm having.

My childish dig stops her dead in her tracks in the center of the main hall with a sharp about-face that nearly topples me into her.

"Are you saying that sleeping with you cost me this job?"

"Were you trying to bed a D'Angelo? Because news flash—the D'Angelos don't fuck the staff."

Ivy recoils, my words hitting her like a slap. It takes her a minute to recover, but she does. "No. Oh my God. No! I would never do that."

Her expression isn't just indignant. It's one of disgust, I think. A new one, for sure, and the polar opposite of the reaction I usually get when I make that accusation.

Still, I fire back. "Of course not. How dare I think that a woman stalking D'Angelo Tower and showing up here today might be trying to get in bed with the D'Angelos."

Hands on her hips, Ivy looks me up and down, her dark eyes flashing as she sizes me up. "There is nothing wrong with what I did yesterday. Checking out a potential employer isn't devious or underhanded. It's smart. And as far as last night goes, looks like I got your name after all, Leo. Leo Zamparelli. The man who fucks a girl one day and holds a gun to her head the next. Look out, ladies. One grade-A dick coming at you."

Without another word, she yanks open the front door and storms out.

I don't even have to look around to know I've got at least a dozen eyes on me. Every one of them belonging to people who technically work for me. Not to mention the ones in the security room, probably zooming in the cameras.

Pinching the bridge of my nose, I say nothing because nothing I can say will make this moment any better. I simply open the credenza, grab a pre-charged burner phone, and follow her.

I step outside and storm after Ivy, ready to draw my weapon again, but this time for an entirely different reason. Andre D'Angelo, or Uncle Andre to the children of this house, has climbed out of his limo and is barreling down the driveway toward her. He's ruthless, deadly, and slick as shit. If we could pin any of the crimes against this family against him, we would. Ivy is no match for the man.

Instead of attacking her, which I completely expect, he's speaking to her. With a hand on her fucking shoulder. If Ivy didn't look shady a second earlier, she sure as hell does now.

"I don't understand," I hear Ivy tell him as I approach

"What did they tell you?" he says so insistently, I intervene.

Andre notices me, and yet, his hand remains firmly on Ivy's shoulder. Like a butterfly whose wings are trapped between his finger and thumb, Ivy has no choice but to struggle aimlessly in his hold. Until he's ready to release her, Ivy isn't going anywhere.

I unbutton my blazer and pocket my hands, giving him full view of my Glock.

Glaring at me, he says, "You'd threaten me? Over her?" His eyes narrow, pinning me with sudden interest. "What's she to you?"

We square off, locked in a stare that determines predator and prey. Finally, he releases her, and I step between them. Shielding her.

"She's a personal guest of Smoke's. One of nearly twenty that will be on the premises today. It's a bad day for you to visit, Andre." *Like the other three hundred sixty-four.* "And your visits are supposed to be scheduled ahead of time and announced."

He dangles a sheet of paper from his fingertips. I snatch it from him, reviewing it as he snarls. "Court order, Z. I have not only the right to access but to seize the property listed."

After skimming the court-issued decree, I hand it back. "It clearly states that the listed items shall be surrendered no later than Friday and says nothing about your access to the home."

"My home. Now, step aside." The odors of seafood and scotch fill the air as he speaks.

Ah, the breakfast of champions.

Despite my kneejerk reaction to back away and take a needed breath, I stand firm. "This is the D'Angelo home. The owner of record is Mason D'Angelo."

Andre scowls. "Smoke stole it from me."

"Too bad the courts don't see it that way. You're leaving, one way or another. A body bag is your call."

Stepping closer, Andre lowers his voice. "Watch out, Leo. Threaten the wrong man, and bad things happen. Who knows? What happened to your wife might happen to your little friend, too."

And just like that, the barrel of my Glock somehow lifts and presses itself between his eyes.

Vaguely, I hear Ivy say my name. A whisper, really, and I half-wonder if I imagined it.

Andre hasn't blinked, and neither have I. It's true, I half-suspect Andre of doing his worst to this family, but no one knows better than I do . . . whatever he did, he didn't do it alone.

Still, my protectiveness shifts into high gear, and it hasn't escaped me that this is the third time I've pulled my weapon in Ivy's presence. Technically, once was at her, but this one should cancel that one out, right?

This girl makes me edgy as hell, and I need to get a fucking grip.

When I speak again, my tone is even and controlled. "See the girl behind me, Andre? Take a good long look at her. Anything happens to her, and I'm going to take it personally. Now, take your court order and your worthless ass off this property."

Glaring daggers at me, he takes three steps back before stomping to the limo behind him. His driver has his door ready, and there's not a doubt that Uncle Andre will be back.

"Have a nice day," I holler for the sheer joy of getting under his skin.

I wait until he's in his car and it's driving away before I holster my weapon. Whatever suspicions I had about her a second ago melt as soon as I see the fear in Ivy's eyes. It's another good reason why she shouldn't be here. The second she drops her keys, I realize she's trembling.

I want to drop my defenses, scoop her into my arms, and take her away from all this. My need to protect her is at direct odds with protecting the D'Angelos. I've learned this the hard way. I can't have both.

Instead, I pick up the keys, moving my hand to the familiar small of her back as I lead her to her car.

As I open the door and help her into her seat, I try not to care. I shouldn't care. I can't care. But when her shaky grip wraps around the steering wheel and a tear slides down her cheek, *fuck*. The solid chunk of ice buried deep within my chest thaws.

"Wait here."

Ivy doesn't look at me, but her small nod is enough.

I race to the house, grab a cup of coffee, water, and a muffin. In the few minutes I've been gone, she hasn't moved.

Opening the passenger door, I take the seat next to her, one I have to slide back so my knees won't be up against my ears. I set the water in the cupholder, the muffin beside it, and place the coffee in her hands.

"Sip," I tell her. It's more of a command than I intend, but she complies. "Andre is just the tip of the iceberg. You think I don't want you here, Ivy? Well, you're right. This place isn't for you. Everything about this world is menacing and dangerous, and I'm the worst of all of it. The man you met last night was an illusion. Here, I'm Z. And the best thing a girl like you can do is head home and never look back."

Either she's pondering my words or she's numb, but she says nothing and doesn't move for a long while. Dredging up patience, I hold my tongue, not pushing her before she's ready. When she does finally speak, her voice is so small, it's all I can do not to hold her.

"Where's their father?"

Her question throws me off. Imagining a world where people don't know what happened to the D'Angelos disturbs me, but it's easy to forget that Ivy isn't from here. That there's a place where the pain that sliced us so deeply had no effect at all.

"Their father passed away."

Saying the words out loud bothers me. More than it should.

And more than it should bother Ivy. I swipe another tear from her cheek, a careless reflex I shouldn't indulge in. Although she doesn't look at me, she doesn't pull away. As soon as the next tear breaks free, I do it again.

I don't know the significance of the event to her, but she holds it in enough reverence that on some level, I understand.

"You lost your father, too?" I ask, and Ivy nods. "I'm sorry."

"Did he die because of the life he led? The life you and Smoke lead now?"

It's then that I realize how naïve Ivy really is to all of this. Her question is too innocent. Too tender.

This is the first time I've talked about this subject to anyone. I've avoided churches for years now, not wanting to go down the path of total hypocrisy. I want to confess but have no intention of apologizing. The sins I've committed are mine. I own them.

But it's good that someone knows the truth. Ivy is as close to a priest as I'll ever come.

Staring out the windshield, I give it to her straight. "Antonio never wanted this life, the life of his father. But the blood of the mafia ran deep through his veins, whether he wanted it or not. It was only a matter of time before they came after him. To this day, we don't know what happened. His body was never found."

"Then how do you know he's dead?" There's hope in her words. The same hope we've all had at one time or another.

"Because Trinity was attacked. If there's one thing I know about Antonio D'Angelo, he'd move heaven and earth to protect his children. He'd never abandon any of them in their time of need."

Ivy turns away, her shoulders lifting with controlled sobs. "And what happens to Trini?" she chokes out. "If I don't come back?"

Ivy's compassion is one I've rarely witnessed. The nurses who tended to my wife were like this, empathetic beyond words. There are those who take and those who give. It's obvious Ivy is a giver.

Another reason my heart reaches out to her. And another reason she can't stay.

I blow out a breath. "We'll find someone else. And Smoke and I will be here. So long as we're around, nothing will happen to her."

"And who looks out for you?"

Her pleading eyes hold mine, and I don't even know how to answer that question. So, I don't.

Holding the cup between us until I take it back, she softly says, "Thanks for the coffee."

I don't want Ivy to go. For once in my life, I want to be open and honest. Actually say what I'm thinking. But I can't. Whatever I would tell her in this moment would become a lie.

I have a job to do, one that includes prying through the lives of suspicious people and their intentions with the D'Angelos. Like Ivy, a girl whose biggest crime so far was agreeing to spend the night with me.

So, I do what I need to do. When Ivy looks away, I drop the cheap cell phone under my seat, its built-in phone-finder app making it a poor man's tracker. Plus, no one bats an eye when we lose a ten-dollar low-tech phone. Lose a sophisticated military-grade tracker, and no fewer than three D'Angelos will seriously lose their shit.

Plus, with a phone, I can eavesdrop. Listen in on any conversation she might have while she's in her car. Because maybe, just maybe, this isn't all a coincidence. She and Andre could be working together. Maybe they have been all along.

It's just a precaution, I tell myself, half-wondering if the paranoia that has served me so well in the past has finally made me crack.

On the other hand, Ivy could be innocent or in a situation where she's in trouble. It's easy to rationalize that this way, I can reach her. At least for the duration of the phone's charge.

I give her a reassuring pat on the hand, or maybe I'm just a psycho who will use any excuse to touch her. Either way, I'm out of reasons to keep sitting here.

Reluctantly, I get out of her car and walk away, casually calibrating the app on my phone to sync to her signal.

CHAPTER 16
Leo

After what feels like six years later, Smoke and I have suffered through interviewing the remaining candidates, including all three men. He looks as exhausted as I feel. "Think it over. We'll figure it out in the morning."

I nod, grab a quick snack from the kitchen, and make my way to my room. Ivy is not only immensely qualified, but her references are impeccable. Even from the d-bag who held the title as her last boss and wants to know if she looks happy.

Really, dude?

And finally, there's the Trinity factor. Ivy isn't just the only outsider to ever crack through Trinity's titanium shield—she's beaten out all of us insiders as well, including me. If she's good enough for Trinity, shouldn't that be all the validation I need?

Trinity is my boss. At least, as much as Smoke or any of the other D'Angelo siblings are. My oath to Antonio hardly came with a pecking order. Between what Smoke knows is best and what Trinity really wants, where do I stand?

Or, as if it matters at all, I have to ask myself . . . what do *I* want?

Ivy's words haunt me. *What if I don't know what I want?* The past couple of years have been a blur. Eat, sleep, work. Or don't eat, don't sleep, work. Work is the only thing keeping me from the spiral of gut-wrenching emptiness. A lifeline that tethers me to some reason—any reason—to keep going.

And if Ivy were here? All I know is I can't keep her close *and* keep her safe.

Life isn't fair. I can choose to protect someone, or I can choose to love someone. No one knows better than I do that I can't have both.

If Ivy were here, how could I not love her? I've known her for such a short time, it's easier to count the time in hours than days, and I'm already falling for her. Picturing her in a white gown with peonies. And as much as she might want a veil, I'd try to talk her out of it because her long, curly hair is too gorgeous to hide. Knowing she'd want nothing too flashy. Something intimate and special and . . .

What the fuck am I thinking?

Before I go into a tailspin of thoughts I shouldn't be having, I do as Smoke recommended. I try to sleep on it. My mind spins as I come up with a million reasons—or just one really, really good one —for why Ivy can't work here.

How about the girl deserves a life? That should work.

So, why can't I sleep?

I toss. I turn. I flip through the stack of books on my nightstand to keep from thinking about what I want. Or from checking her location.

Taking three cold showers in some deranged attempt to kill off thoughts of the naked curves of her body is pointless. No matter how much I try to turn it off, my brain is intent on retracing every lickable inch.

Maybe I should man up. Admit up front that Ivy can't work here because my self-control is shot. That should keep her from being hired, right?

The chill of my current shower is my sanctuary. There's something about a torrent of ice-cold water against the skin of a former Navy SEAL that clears my head. Helps me think. It also helps stave off a raging boner. Win-win.

When I return to bed, I chart the thirty cutouts in the coffered ceiling of my bedroom over and over again because the bottom line is I can't sleep on it. I can't sleep at all. With the loss of her credit card and the condition of her car, who knows where she's sleeping tonight. Is she safe? I don't know why I care about this, but I obviously do.

Knock. Knock-knock.

With only a half dozen people living under this roof, I've made a game out of predicting who's behind the door before I answer it. Even though I'm positive I know who the person is standing on the other side, it's not because I've ever heard this knock. It's because I haven't.

I scramble to my feet and slip on a pair of sweatpants and yank a PROPERTY OF US NAVY T-shirt over my head. Then I flip on the soft amber light from the nightstand.

"Come in, Trinity."

When Trinity opens the door, she doesn't enter right away. Fidgeting with the hem of her sweatshirt that reads HOME IS WHERE THE CANNOLI IS, she stares at me curiously with big blue eyes. "How did you know it was me?"

"Lucky guess," I say with a smile, welcoming her into an area of the mansion she hasn't seen in years. I'm glad she's seeing it. It is her house, after all.

She surveys the room, nodding in silent approval of what I've done since she last saw it. Probably grateful that I've avoided an oversaturation of flannel or marring the wall with a deer's head.

My stance is as casual as it can be at military parade rest. It was how I always stood when her father visited . . . which he did whenever he needed to offload a secret or two. Like possible locations for the family's holiday vacation. Or how to cut ties with Andre.

"I'm sorry I'm dropping by so late."

Smiling at her, I say, "It's all right. I wasn't sleeping."

I gesture to an oversized leather chair, one with a throw pillow featuring an adorable labradoodle mix that Trinity gave me several Christmases ago. An embroidered rendition of my childhood dog, Noble, that she designed from a photo I have at the corner of my desk, next to a few other priceless memories.

When Trinity sits, she pulls up her feet and hugs the pillow against her chest. It reminds me of the old Trinity, and my smile widens.

"It's never too late. What's on your mind?"

Her brow creases, making me more attentive. "Why did you pull a gun on Ivy?"

As I draw in a long, thoughtful breath, I figure out what to say. Nothing I say can explain why I might have pegged Ivy as a threat when Trinity had such an instant affinity for her.

Scratch that. We both had an instant affinity for her.

Shrugging, I level with her. "Sometimes my training overrides my good judgment."

"So, you didn't pull the weapon on her because of your good judgment?"

I want to say something profound, like *only time will tell*, but even in my head, I sound like an asshole. Instead, I double down on a girl I barely know. "No. Just a knee-jerk reaction. I'm hardwired to protect you. Old habits die hard."

"Smoke offered her the job," Trinity says, watching me carefully.

Stunned, I struggle to keep my emotions to myself.

That's so very like him. Giving me some bullshit line about how *we'll think it over* when he's already made up his fucking mind. Probably hoped I would come around. Bring it up to him at breakfast like it was my idea. *Fucker.*

But now, I wonder. Why is Trinity here? "Doesn't that make you happy? You seem to have taken to her."

"She turned it down."

There's no hiding my surprise when I hear that. Elbows on my knees, I steeple my fingers and lean in. "Did she give a reason?"

"No. I was wondering if you might know."

Trinity's statement could be accusatory. I mean, I did pull a gun on the woman. But it's not. In fact, there's hope in Trinity's inquisitive gaze. She wants me to have an answer that I don't have. Or maybe I do.

I could fess up, admit that I talked Ivy out of it. But something tells me that wasn't the reason she turned down the job. I don't think my little pep talk would have kept her from this if she really wanted it. Ivy was genuinely concerned for Trinity.

It could be all that bullshit with Uncle Andre. Hell, the thought of confronting a bastard like him has made half the high-powered men in Chicago squirm. No one could expect Ivy to take it on the chin and power through.

Or it could be me?

The thought of working day in and day out with the man she had a one-night stand with. We were both exceptionally clear. No commitments. Or at least, she didn't want one.

An uncomfortable knot forms in the pit of my stomach.

What if it *was* me? The real me. The one who stuck the business end of a pistol at another man's head and didn't think twice. The man who's above redemption but not revenge. For many men, I'm the monster in their nightmares. Maybe I'm Ivy's as well.

With Trinity's gentle gaze trained on me, I try to shrug it off.

Which leads her to ask, "Can I hire you?"

I let out a modest chuckle before I speak. "I already work for you."

"You work for Smoke."

"I work for all of Antonio's children. And the last time I checked, you were one of them. So, to answer your question, no. You can't hire me. But I am at your disposal for anything you need."

"I want you to find her. Find out why she's not taking the job."

If it were anyone else asking, this would be the end of the conversation. Hard pass. Hell no.

But this is Trinity. The woman who's said more words to me today than in the past four years.

"Of course. But I do need payment from you. In the form of information."

Her bright eyes widen. "Anything. What do you want to know?"

"Why is Ivy so important to you?" I ask.

She shrugs, thinking on the question. "You and Smoke look at me like I'm made of glass. And I know it's because I'm fragile. There are times I'm so close to shattering—"

"Trinity . . . " I was trained well enough that I don't try to hug her. But still, I reach out.

"She saw me staring at the little swan, trapped in the reeds. She asked if we should save it. *We*. And it was like a light turned on. I can't change what happened. But maybe I can reclaim tiny pieces of life." She smiles thoughtfully. "One baby swan rescue at a time."

I choke back a tear. "I saw how you set up a little area for it out back. Did you name it?"

"Ivy calls her Fluff."

I can't help nodding. "Sounds perfect." Trinity shifts, and I notice her pocket. "Food?" I ask, pointing to it and imaging her smuggling some bread to the baby swan.

Shyly, she pulls a little furry bundle from the pocket of her pink plaid pajama pants. It's Ivy's stuffed animal. Reluctantly, Trinity hands him over.

"I had a bunch of these when I was younger. Nonna gave them to me. They came in a set of a dozen. I'm sure they were in every big-box store at the time. The set had lots of cats and dogs, an elephant, a pony, and a baby chick. My brothers were always hiding them from me, but that one was my favorite. I don't think she meant for me to keep it."

Ivy was right. Mr. Whiskers does make me feel better. Holding the plush little toy and gazing into its permanently happy face, I can't stop a smile from forming.

"She calls him Mr. Whiskers," I tell Trinity as I tap his little nose. Next thing you know, I'll be introducing him to Noble. But pretend-animal tea parties is where I draw the line.

Trinity pins me with those earnest blue eyes. "Can you find her? I just want to talk with her. If she doesn't want the job, I understand. But I'd like to know why she turned it down. Or at the very least, get Mr. Whiskers back to her."

That could be a really bad idea, but I'm not about to tell Trinity that. Without a word, I nod my answer.

"Good," she says, popping to her feet with way too much energy for the wee hours of the morning.

I head to the door and open it for her but take a deliberate step back, not wanting to intrude on her space. "It's really good talking with you, Trinity."

"Good night, Z."

Taking a seat in the chair she just sat in, I pull that same dog pillow to my lap and stare in disbelief at the other personality in the room.

"Did that really happen?" I ask Mr. Whiskers expectantly. He says nothing and simply stares. "And now I'm supposed to go after her?" Again, nothing. I give the little toy a goofy-ass grin. "Fine. Let's go find her."

I scoop the little toy into my hand, but the second I squeeze, *crunch*.

Flipping the little guy to fully expose his furry backside, I find a zipper that loops around the base of him. The zipper is small, revealing a hidden compartment stuffed with cash. Fanned out, the money equates to roughly everything she had in her purse when we met.

Worried as hell, I grab my cell and activate the phone-finder app.

Ivy's in a strange city with no credit card, no cash, and possibly nowhere to sleep tonight except her car. Fuck, without money, her options are to sleep parked on the side of the road or in a chain-store parking lot.

Or what if she tried going home, thinking she had cash? Tried, and then ran out of gas, stranded halfway between here and North Carolina? The tank of gas she's left with won't even get her halfway home.

Shit.

The little dot finally gets a lock on her. The car isn't moving. Based on the tracker's history, the car hasn't budged in the past three hours.

And it's in the last damn place Ivy should be.

CHAPTER 17
Ivy

"Time to wake up."

The woman's voice jolts me, and I lurch to sit up straight, though she's not particularly loud or menacing.

Her guard uniform is professional but snug, an odd complement to her lack of makeup and tightly wound bun. Her nameplate is a blur, and I rub my eyes to read it in the low light. Her last name is Stefano, I think. In all honesty, she looks like my mother. So much like her, I have to strain my eyes to make certain the woman I'm seeing isn't her.

I wasn't sleeping, though I don't say so. And it wasn't because the mattress is paper-thin or that the wool blanket feels like steel wool against my skin, an allergy I've never outgrown.

No, a dozen other things were keeping me wide awake.

The dark gray walls that inch closer with every breath. The echoes of every noise as the smallest sounds cut through the air as unrelenting explosions. The soul-draining bars that steal my freedom, and the stainless steel toilet that faces them.

But most of all, the biggest reason I wasn't sleeping a wink is that I wanted to know *why*. Why was I pulled over when I was technically under the speed limit? Why was I arrested? No phone call. No lawyer. No answers. The only rational thought I cling to is to remain calm because lashing out only makes it worse.

"You made bail."

Bail? Did Aunt Grace figure out I was here? Did someone call her? Mortified, I step out of the cell. Aunt Grace is probably full of worry and questions, and in a lot of ways, so am I.

I'm no stranger to police stations. It's how Brooke and I met. In the lobby, not a cell, though we love telling people we met in the slammer.

People always checked in on me when I was younger, and for a lot of years, I resented it. Having a deputy pick me up because my mom left me again was humiliating.

Most of the time, I had plenty of cereal and milk and Mr. Whiskers. But Deputy Everly took me to the sheriff's office and sat me next to his desk and always gave me half of the sandwich his wife had made him for lunch. Sometimes, Mrs. Everly would bring Brooke to visit when I was there, along with homemade pie. And Brooke always left me with a Twinkie.

Say what you will about those golden cakes, they are my comfort food. I'd give almost anything for a Twinkie right now.

The guard leads me to an area where I collect my belongings, the sum total of which isn't much. Car keys, my smartphone, and a wallet with nothing more than my driver's license are the bulk of my worldly possessions at the moment.

I pocket them, and as quickly as I was arrested, I'm released. When the solid door clanks shut behind me, I just want is to go home. Home-home. Not Aunt Grace's, though I love her more than bacon. But Chicago has been nothing but a curse, and all I want is my comforter, my favorite mug filled with cocoa, and to forget the past few days ever happened.

The lobby is empty except for one man. His jeans are worn and look more comfortable than he deserves. And as good as he looks in a fitted dark T-shirt that serves to expand his shoulders and amplify every muscle in his chest, I ignore it.

Or I try to, anyway, because I'm furious.

Not furious enough to cause a scene in the middle of a police precinct where I might wind up back in a cell, but angry enough to avoid his bright blue eyes. I shake my head in disgust, pushing past him to head straight for the exit.

Leo's footsteps follow behind mine. "You're welcome," he has the audacity to say as if *I* should be thanking *him*.

Stay calm. But I can't stay calm. I'm cold, I'm tired, Leo's body is so close there's nothing but masculine-smelling him all around me, and I have no idea where my goddamn car is.

Shit.

I step outside and press the button on my key fob like crazy, hoping to hear the familiar honk of my car, when Leo rushes past me, blocking me from moving any farther.

"You wanna give me a second, considering I just sprang you from jail?"

"So, you have me thrown in jail, have a little fun at my expense, then become bored enough with whatever sadistic game it is you're playing and finally have me released. And now you deserve my thanks?" My words are pained and slow, threatening in the most juvenile way.

But when Leo looks at me, pleading with those crystal-blue eyes, my knee is ten seconds from kicking his balls clear to his eyebrows.

His eyes widen as if he's read my mind. Intelligently, he takes a step back.

Raising his hands, he breathes out his nose as if he does this meditation exercise regularly, careful in selecting his words. "I didn't put you in jail. That would be the charming Uncle Andre you met earlier."

Desperate for an answer, I fire back. "No one would tell me what I was being charged with."

He replies through gritted teeth, tight-jawed and angered. "Because they don't have to." He steps closer, demanding my attention. Pained, his eyes hold mine. "They can hold you for forty-eight hours. Sometimes seventy-two. And not charge you at all."

Rage boils below the surface, but I breathe through it and stay calm. Determined not to lash out or cry, I march away. Leo's voice follows. "I discovered where you were, and I bailed you out . . . with my own money," he hollers after me.

I ignore him, frantically clicking the button on my fob. *Click-click-click-click-click.*

"It's no use looking for your car."

Now I see red. That car is barely worth the price of the dinner he took me out to, but it's all I have.

Before I can tear into Leo, he explains. "It's in impound. They don't open for a few more hours."

Tears prick the back of my eyes. I'm out of jail, but there's nowhere I can go. He bailed me out, knowing I'd be stranded. I'm helpless, but I can't give him the satisfaction of crying. I won't.

Finding a small area of curb, I take a seat. "Then I'll wait."

Leo should leave. Why isn't he leaving?

I turn on my phone, intent on making the most of the wait. As soon as it flashes on, my battery is red. Nineteen percent. Enough for at least a phone call.

I need to think. At this point, my only option is Aunt Grace. My thumb hovers over her number, but I can't press it. I can't. The thought of her big, worried eyes pitying me. It's too much. That, coupled with the blood pressure medication she's been skimping on, makes calling her completely out of the question.

The phone flashes. Eighteen percent. I click it off, then pull my knees up enough to rest my head on them.

"What's going on between you and Andre?"

I'm not even going to pretend to understand what Leo's asking me. Ignoring his accusation, or jealousy, or whatever the hell he asked, I lay into him. "I don't want you here, and I don't need you here. Go away, Leo. Get out of my life, and leave me alone." My voice is muffled, and I keep my face down, letting the tears fall against the leg of my jeans.

"This isn't about me, Ivy. If I had my way, you would've been long gone yesterday."

Oh my God, really? What an asshole.

"But I can't leave yet," he says, his words way too tender for me to deal with now.

From beneath my lashes, I watch his big dumb shoes saunter over, then stop right in front of me before he turns and sits down next to me. I'm edgy and irritated but too worn out to fight. When his warm hand lands on my shoulder, I sit up, tears and all, ready to tell him to fuck off. It's either that or cry on his shoulder, and I can't.

He said it himself. If it were up to him, I'd be gone.

Instead, I just ask, "What do you want from me, Leo?"

"Andre isn't your friend."

"Gee, what gave it away?"

"He's been after the D'Angelo estate ever since Antonio died. I promise you, if he's trying to get close to you, it's only to hurt them."

What? Does Andre know? That I'm really a D'Angelo?

I swipe away a few stubborn tears and look up at him, studying Leo's expression. His eyes.

I hadn't noticed his hand until now. He holds Mr. Whiskers at eye level, leaving his palm open until I take it.

"If you take the job—you'll be under our protection. You'll live on the estate, have security around the clock, and a car at your disposal. Smoke made you a generous offer, and under the circumstances, I've been authorized to double it. Trinity wants you to stay."

Silently, my eyes search his. *What about you, Leo? Do you want me to stay?*

I ask these questions in my head, idiotically wanting him to say the exact opposite of what he actually said just a few minutes ago.

Wiping a tear with Mr. Whiskers, I say, "I need to think about it."

I've been offered a job that's more than I've ever wanted. Close to the family I desperately want to know. Doing exactly what I love. At twice the rate of what was already a huge raise over the job I just left. But my words come out emotionless. All I feel is numb.

"That's understandable." Leo stands as if getting ready to leave. "Take all the time you need. I'll be right over there." He points to a lone sports car parked thirty feet from us.

Is he deranged? "I'm going to need more than five minutes."

"I understand. But until you decide, I'll be watching out for you. I'm not always Z, chief of security for the D'Angelos, protector of their interests. Sometimes I'm just Leo. If you decide to take the position, I go back to my security role."

Is he saying I'm just another one of their interests?

"And if I pass? Return home?"

"Then I'll look out for you from afar until I know you're safe."

This coming from the man who, minutes ago, said he wanted me to leave. I have no idea what he's trying to say, but now, on top of being tired and cold, I'm angry. I snap to my feet, infuriated. "Oh, no, you don't."

He crosses his arms. "No, I don't, what?"

"You don't get to pretend to give two shits about me and still play the good guy."

"The offer to stay is from Smoke. Not me. And the option to leave is for your own goddamned good. And for the record, I never said I was the good guy. In fact, I'm not the good guy. I'm a living fucking nightmare, and someone you should stay far away from."

"I storm up to him, glaring face-to-face. "Then. Leave."

"I can't."

"Why not?"

He growls, fighting whatever it is he wants to say. Finally, he huffs out. "Because you're not safe."

I throw my hands in the air. "I'm in front of a police station, Leo. But suit yourself."

I take in my surroundings. Creepy street one way. Equally creepy street the other way with the sign pointing to the impound lot. I march off in the lesser of the scary directions and head to the destination holding my car.

"Where are you going?" he hollers.

I have no fucking idea. "The hell away from you," I shout back.

Half a block down the road, my heartbeat jumps as a car pulls up beside me. Shivering, I'm praying it's a cop because the cell was definitely warmer than this.

"Get in the car," Leo orders.

Eyes forward, I keep walking.

The car rolls to a stop ahead of me. Leo steps out, brooding and moody, determined to block my path.

In an instant, I hate him. And I want him.

"Get in the car."

I stand my ground. "No."

Now it's his turn to step into my space. I meet the fury in his eyes with a defiant glare. Lowering his voice, he says it again. "Get in the car."

I knot my arms in front of my chest.

"Stop fighting me, Ivy. You're not safe out here. I'm trying to protect you."

"Why?" I snap. He stares. So, I ask him again. "Why, Leo? Why are you here? Why do you want me safe? Why are you so hell-bent on protecting me?"

He grabs my face. "Because bad things happen to everyone I care about, and I care about you."

He grabs my face and kisses me. A slow, sweeping kiss that liquifies me. I don't want Leo Zamparelli. I *need* him. My heart squeezes when I think that in some small way, maybe he needs me, too.

His grip on my face tightens as lips crush mine. His tongue rushes through with sweeping, tender strokes. Dizzy, I melt into him. He stops kissing me, but he doesn't let go.

"I can't be in a relationship, Ivy, and not because I don't want to be. Because I can't. I gave a dying man my word that I'd always protect his family. Given the choice between my job and my love life, my job comes first. Always. If you stay, our relationship will be nothing but professional. It has to be. I can't protect you if I—"

He cuts himself off, and I ache to know what he was going to say.

If you what, Leo?

But a wall goes back up, and he continues as if he wasn't about to share something important.

"If you go, at least I have the peace of mind to know you'll be safe, but any relationship we would have had no longer exists. But here—in the twilight between those two decisions—I'm here for you, in a way I can never be once you decide. I meant what I said. Take your time. I'm in no rush for you to race to one extreme or the other."

Leo moves back to his car to open the passenger door, and I feel shattered by his words.

He didn't say, "I want to be the man in your life," so why does it feel like he did? And why is the decision so impossible?

I get it. Staying is risky. Andre is probably just one in a long line of ruthless men used to getting what they want, even by force. And Antonio D'Angelo is gone. Any hope I have to meet my father died a long time ago.

And then there's Leo. Could I really work side by side with the man and pretend there's nothing between us?

But if I go, I'll never know the family that's mine. All these years, I've thought I was an only child. But I'm not. I have six brothers, and if the rest of them are even half as interesting as Smoke, how could I not want to get to know them?

Plus, I have a sister. A sister who probably needs me in a way I've never been needed before. How can I turn my back on Trinity?

I rub the soft fur of Mr. Whiskers with my thumb, feeling the line of the zipper. I didn't just hide my money in here after my purse was nearly stolen. I hid a precious piece of my life.

Curious, I unzip it. All the cash is there, but the photo is gone.

Did Leo take it? Is that why he's saying this? Or did Trinity? Who else held my small childhood friend in the palm of their hand?

It doesn't matter. Sighing, I zip him back up and think about what I really want.

My steps are contemplative as I walk over to Leo. But as soon as I approach, Leo takes a long moment to study me. "You've made a decision."

I nod.

He reads me, deciphering my thoughts. His hand is warm on my cheek, and I lean into it. "You're sure."

"Yes."

Moving my hands up his chest and around his neck, I pull his lips to mine. In the same way I'm giving in to everything I want and need in this moment, so is Leo. Our kiss is rough and free, and I take as much from him as he does from me.

"I know what I want," I whisper, adding, "no commitments," giving him the permission he needs to take me somewhere. Anywhere.

"No commitments," he murmurs back against my mouth.

Leo drives for half an hour to a wooded area that opens to a small field. Beneath a velvety star-filled sky, he ushers me out of the car, retrieves a soft blanket from the trunk, and lays it on the hood.

"I can take you somewhere else," he says, uncertainty flickering behind the heat in his eyes. "But when the sun rises from this spot, there's nothing like it."

"It's perfect."

"You're perfect," he says, landing kisses on my mouth and neck, and I waste no time peeling his clothes from him as he unbuttons my jeans. "Turn around."

I smile through the kisses sweeping over my lips. "But I want to watch you come."

He wraps my hair in his fist, making a tingle shoot to my core. "You will, beautiful. I promise, you will."

Leo strips my remaining clothes from me, and I turn around, letting him once again command me. He controls my body in ways that slowly unravel me, and it's everything.

With his hand against my back, he presses soft open-mouthed kisses along my spine as I'm facedown against the soft blanket, warmed by the heat of the engine. When he buries his face inside me from behind, I lose my breath, crying loud and free to the darkness and the sky.

Sensations sweep over me. His tongue. His finger slowly circling my clit, torturing me. The heat of his breath panting into me. All I want is to bottle up this moment so I can revisit it again and again and again.

When I shatter, it's into a billion pieces of ecstasy that remind me of everything that happened between us our first night together. Leo is unlike any man I've ever known, and my body burns, craving more of him. I have to see him.

The dark sky is just beginning to lighten along the horizon as he rolls me over. He slides the head of his dick along me, working the tip in place, then stops.

Realizing why, I tighten my legs around his waist. "I'm on the pill."

Even with glimpses of sunlight working their way over the horizon, there's no denying the blaze in his expression. "You sure?"

"Yes."

I've barely breathed out the word when he enters me, shredding me with one hard thrust. "Leo."

Breathless, I throw my head back as he pounds into me hard and fast. Nothing gentle or tame. No remorse. No regret.

The man I met the other night went easy on me, but this man, this man forces me to take all of him, hating me in one thrust and worshiping me with the next.

And all I can do is spread wider, arch my back, and beg because I want more. "Please, Leo. Please."

"Come for me, baby."

And just like that, I do. We do. Locking our eyes. Our souls. Colliding into each other as our climaxes hit us both at once.

And then it's over. As we hold each other, catching our breath, the sun comes up. The world is more beautiful and yet emptier all at once.

Without speaking, we dress, and when he returns me to the car, Leo is gentle. Caring.

I wonder what it would be like, a life with this side of Leo. Because I'm not naive. A life with Z would never be possible.

"I need to talk with Trinity," I say softly, and he only nods.

The drive to the estate is long. For the most part, the silence is filled with music from a local AM station, which gives more reality of the world around us rather than an escape.

Leo shuts off the radio and glances at me. "Yesterday was the first time Trinity has spoken to me in four years."

The shock of that statement steals my breath.

"Why?" I ask, wrestling to make sense of his words.

Leo brings his hand gently over mine. "Trinity was attacked four years ago."

Some part of me suspected that, though I didn't know the specifics.

"It was brutal," he says, pain lacing his words. "She was left for dead, an act that shattered the family. The attack happened shortly after her father's death. It's rare that she speaks to anyone. Anyone except Smoke."

That doesn't make any sense. "But she was talking. We were talking."

"About what?" Leo gives me a curious glance, wanting to know the secrets of a puzzle that isn't always meant to be comprehended.

I don't have a good answer for him. "I introduced myself, but she seemed more interested in Mr. Whiskers, so I introduced him as well. Like I usually do with a new client, I handed him to her and walked away, letting her have a moment with him when I wasn't looking. That way she didn't feel compelled to keep up the conversation."

Leo frowns, obviously dissatisfied with my answer. "What else did you talk about?"

"Hair, mostly. She loved the color of my hair, especially this." I loop my finger around the long silvery curl that most people think is dyed to look that way.

Leo dons that confused-man expression, the one all men wear when the social customs of women don't compute. "There has to be more."

"There was," I say to explain. "Fluff. She could see the baby swan was stuck. And ... you saw the rest."

By the tight line of his lip and the clench to his jaw, my explanation seems unsatisfying. "Are you sure that's all?"

Am I sure that's all we got to before a gun was pulled on me?

"Yes," I say, keeping the rest to myself. "That's all."

Silence settles between us again, and whatever connection we shared moments ago fades like smoke on a breeze. The closer we get to the D'Angelo estate, the farther I feel from Leo.

Or perhaps this is Z.

By the time we arrive at the estate, Trinity waits to greet us, and I can't believe how happy I am to see her again. She's at the door before Leo comes to a complete stop, and as soon as he does, I open the door.

"I'm so glad you've decided to stay," she says.

"Ivy has something to tell you," Leo says, giving me a pointed look.

I can practically read his mind. He seems ready for me to let Trinity down gently. If that's what he's thinking, he's in for a surprise.

"Me, too," I say, giving her a slight hug that she leans into more than I anticipated, stealing my breath.

Based on Leo's expression, my answer is unexpected.

Hands on his hips, he cocks his head. "I thought you were leaving."

"I never said that."

"A word." Leo isn't asking. His large hand wraps around my arm as he gently but firmly pulls me aside.

I give him innocent eyes and a cool smile. "I said I'd made a decision."

"You said no commitments. As in, *C'est la vie. 'Bye, Leo. Not seeing you again.*"

"No, I said no commitments as a reminder. If we're going to be working side by side, day in and day out, and you're a man who doesn't do relationships, it's better for both of us that we keep that little mantra at the forefront. No. Commitments."

His nostrils flare, and he crosses his arms. Mine cross, too, but he can see I'm amused. There's a smile that threatens, but he doesn't give in.

"You know the reasons it's dangerous for you to stay."

"I know."

He reaches for me, his hands locking on my arms, fire in his expression. Before he can say more—or kiss me—or do whatever a broody alpha male does in situations that are completely beyond their control, Trinity breaks in.

"Is everything all right?"

"No," he shouts, boiling over before he pumps the brakes and simmers down. Calmer now, he says, "This isn't your call or my call or Ivy's call."

"Then whose call is it, Leo?" I ask, my turn to pop my hands on my hips.

He storms off, saying sharply over his shoulder, "It's Smoke's."

CHAPTER 18

Leo

I hear Ivy's small steps rush after me, so I pick up the pace. To be honest, pinning the decision on Smoke is a desperate play. I'm grasping at straws, but the woman has turned my world upside down, and she hasn't even moved in.

I knock once, loud, as I barge in. "I need to speak with you."

Smoke looks at me warily from behind his desk. "I'll have to call you back," he says from his phone.

"She can't stay," I insist.

"Why not?" Smoke asks.

Ivy knocks once and charges in behind me. "Yes, why not?"

Turning to face her, I say, "You can't just barge in here."

Smoke rolls his eyes. Hands clasped across his chest, he leans back into his chair. "Do I need a gavel?"

Frustrated, I plant my hands on Smoke's desk and lean in. "Her background check isn't finished."

"I've lived in North Carolina all my life. My best friend's father is the sheriff." Well, that's just great. And fucking convincing.

Smoke passes an imperceivable glance her way, and I know he's swayed. *Shit.* He tosses me a look, and I can already read his mind. But his words surprise me. "Give us a minute, Ivy."

"But—" This time, his look is sterner, and she complies. "Okay," she says meekly.

We both watch as she walks out the door. The second she shuts it I can breathe.

"Well?" Smoke asks.

"Well, what?"

"Why can't she stay? Because you're horny?"

I deadpan.

"Maybe you need a vacation, Leo. A break."

I scoff. "Please. Without me around, you couldn't find your nuts to scratch them. Seriously, there's no one who will bother to point them out to you."

He offers me a seat which I reluctantly take. From the fridge, he tosses me a coke, while he pours himself a scotch. "No one— not you—not me—have gotten through to Trinity. It's the break-through of the fucking millennium."

"Her being here is dangerous. She's on Andre's radar."

His face contorts with suspicion. "Why?"

"I don't know. Yet," I add. "But I'll find out."

He stares out the window, taking a long sip of his drink. "Then keeping her around makes it that much easier to find out."

Unsettled, I exhale. Loud.

"Tell me I'm wrong," he challenges, and that's just it. He's not wrong.

"Just breathing over here. Isn't a man allowed to breathe?"

"Yup," he says with another sip before turning to me. "The choice is yours, Leo."

"What?" *Where did that come from?* I stand. "What do you mean the choice is mine? After going on about what an asset she is to Trini and that she might be a strategic advantage against Andre. Now, all of a sudden, the choice is mine? The hell it is."

"Half the time, the two of you are in some weird tango between hating each other and fucking each other, and as much as my morbid curiosity wants to keep Ivy around just to see how your little love-hate-fuck fest ends, it's not my life, Leo. It's yours. She'll be reporting to you. Working for you. Day in and day out."

He takes a moment to stare at a photo of Trini, weighing the consequences of what he's saying. "We all know what you've been through, Leo. This can't be my decision or Trini's. It's yours."

I want to tell him I'd do anything for Trini. For him. For this family. And it claws at my heart that I can't.

He tosses back the rest of his drink, centering the glass on his desk. "Let her know which way you decide. We're behind you, Leo. One hundred percent." He pats my back. "We're family."

He walks out. And I'm left wondering what the hell I do now.

CHAPTER 19
Leo

"Well?" I eavesdrop, hearing Ivy grill Smoke as he enters the hall. I open the door wide enough to see Trini standing beside Ivy, holding her goddamned hand.

"Well, what?" he replies as if unconcerned.

Ivy seems prepared to ease off from his callous response. Trinity has no such patience and socks him in the arm. Pleasantly, I'm surprised. "Ow," Smoke winces with a chuckle as he rubs his arm. My heart squeezes. The old Trini is back.

"Smoke?" Ivy whines sweetly. "Please, just tell me."

He shakes his head. "I can't."

Trini slumps her shoulders, disappointed. "Why not?" she asks.

It's apparent he has no good answer, and neither do I. Nonetheless, he's ready to have my back. Cover for the decision he's sure I've settled on. Looking between the two of them, he covers his emotions. Poker face up, he starts. "Because—"

"Because the person who will be hired into the position reports to me," I say, entering the hall.

Smoke wraps an arm around Trinity. "How about you and I go feed your swan?"

Thoughtfully, I rub my scruff. "It might be best if Trinity hears this, too, Smoke."

He hugs her a tiny bit tighter, ever the watchful brother. "Are you sure about that?"

Smoke flashes me an uncertain look, and for the first time, I'm pretty sure I see fear in that son of a bitch's eyes. Good. After the landmine of emotion he just put me through, soak in the payback, butthead.

I face Ivy. "There are inherent risks in the job you would be accepting."

"I know," she says, nodding.

"You'll have to sign away any and all forms of liability. Non-disclosure agreements. Getting sued will be the least of your worries if you violate the terms."

My threat lands undetonated. "I understand."

"Your background check will be extensive. Anyone who's ever known you will be interviewed. Family. Friends. Ex-boyfriends."

She swallows hard, and Trini lights up, filled with hope.

"You'd be required to live on the property. Be available to Trinity twenty-four seven. And your employment will involve peeing in a cup on a fairly regular basis."

Ivy blinks. "Please tell me that's for a drug screening and not a fetish."

I palm my face.

"Does this mean I have the job?"

I look at her and then at Trini and question my sanity. It was going to be easy. Tell her we've made another selection. Anything to get her the hell away from here and off the property. But between her big eyes and Trini's, I can't do it. But I can't just offer her the job. I won't.

"It means you'll be on a probationary period. For a month. Maybe longer. You can be fired for any reason at any time. No questions asked."

The two women squeal like schoolgirls as I settle into the decision I'll probably regret. Smoke keeps his eyes on me, expressive in both his hopes and doubts. Like every other day around here, I ignore him.

"You'll sign your paperwork now," I say flatly. "Your employment starts first thing in the morning.

"But you can stay tonight," Trini offers, and what the hell can I say? I can't stop her from having Ivy over as a guest.

Unsettled, I have one more thing to say to Ivy. In private. "The documents are waiting in Smoke's office." Addressing Trini, I add, "She'll catch up with you in a minute."

Smoke leads Trini in the opposite direction as Ivy and I make our way back to Smoke's office. Once inside, I shut the door. "Where are the papers?" she asks, looking around on the desk.

I step around to Smoke's side, using the desk to put some needed distance between us. I slide several sheets toward her, along with a pen. She begins to sign as I give her a solemn warning. "If there's anything you're hiding—anything at all, now is the time to tell me."

The long line of her signature stops. And there's that swallow again. I wait out whatever she's thinking through.

I half-expect a confession when she flips the page and signs the next block. "I understand," she says quietly. My job—my life—is reading people. But with Ivy, I can't, and it bugs the shit out of me.

Watching her, it's hard to tell if she's hiding something or engrossed in reading. I double down on my instincts. There's something there. Something she doesn't want me to know. Maybe it's about her. Maybe it's about Andre. Or maybe it's about me, settling one arm comfortably into the snug warmth of a straitjacket. Nevertheless, I reiterate my point. "This is your chance to come clean."

She ignores me.

"What we do is dangerous." I remind her, leaning in. She doesn't respond. My hand lands on the pages she's engrossed in.

"I've killed people, Ivy." Doe-eyed, she looks up at me. "Too many to count."

She blinks. "You're an ex-SEAL working for a family related to the mob," she says with a silent *duh*. Why is it when she says it like that, it doesn't sound so bad?

I hit her with the other thing weighing on me. "You also understand we can't have a relationship."

This time, her signing doesn't stop. If anything, she speeds up, one signature after another like a gold medal's on the line. "I understand," she says. At the rate she's going, she'll be done signing in under a minute.

Irritated that she suddenly needs to rush out of here and not challenge me at all on the subject, I pocket my hands. "Nothing but professional." I wait for her argument.

"Professional," she repeats, signing the last of the pages and setting down the pen. She turns and heads for the door.

"You didn't read anything. You just signed."

"I trust you."

Well, that seems like a big fucking mistake considering I just told her I kill people. "We're not finished yet," I say with enough authority, she stops in her tracks and spins in place.

"I am." She checks her watch. "I don't start working for you immediately. Not until tomorrow. So right now, I'm going to go feed Fluff."

She walks out, and I stand there and stew before marching straight to the door. Boiling over, I shout, "That goose is going to get as big as fucking Godzilla the way you two keep feeding it."

Dignified, she shouts back, "It's a swan."

I whip out my phone. "Siri!" I bark.

"Siri here."

"What the fuck is a swan?"

CHAPTER 20

Ivy

I burst from the door and into the hall, heart pounding so hard I can't breathe. My feet move ahead of me as I struggle to keep my composure. *He knows.*

Leo had me sign a stack of papers written in Greek just so he can nail me to the wall.

The more distance I put between Leo and me, the better I feel. My rational thought returns. No, there's no way he could know. *How could he know who I am? Even I don't know who I am. Not officially.*

I find a quiet corner of the kitchen. I need the equivalent of human Valium. My fingers dial Aunt Grace. From the window, I watch as Smoke holds Fluff while Trini feeds her. "Leo's right," I say to myself, smiling. "We've really got to stop feeding that much food to Fluff."

The phone only rings once. "Ivy. Thank goodness you called. I was starting to worry. Were you with your Hottie McGoddie?" she asks.

I wish. "Actually, I got the job. And I'll be living on the property."

"That's so exciting, though you will still have to visit on your days off." And for the second time, Leo's right. I should have read the fine print. Do I even get time off? "And this gives you more time to look for your father." My father. Everything happened so fast. I never got to tell her that I did find him. About five years too late.

"Yes," I say with the heavy weight of sadness. "Find my father —" The second the words leave my mouth, I notice Leo. His dark eyes hold mine as he steps closer. Did he hear what I just said? My heart pounds a mile a minute as he steps my way. "I have to go," I say into the phone.

"All right, Ivy-vine. Love you." It's how she always says goodbye if she thinks it'll be a while before she sees me again. It won't be. I'm an hour away and can be there in no time.

Still, I say it back. "Love you, too." I smile sadly, hearing the line disconnect.

Leo steps into my space, broody and sullen. I haven't the foggiest clue what he's thinking, but it feels like a barrier between us. Did he put two and two together? His eyes lock on mine. Maybe something came up in the background investigation.

The harder he stares, the more I tense. Is he going to kick me out?

Still, there's a chance he doesn't know, and my heart races with indecision. Sooner or later, I have to tell him. This is my chance to come clean. Tell him the truth. From the moment we met, I was looking for my father. Smoke might be my brother. Trini might be my sister.

Purge the enormity of the secret between us. And then what?

You're right, Leo. I *was* stalking D'Angelo Tower, but not in a bad way. And I managed to wedge myself into the trust and home of a family worth billions, but it's not about the money.

Losing myself in his darkening eyes, I take in a sharp breath, ready to tell him. Now.

Before I overthink it, I force it out. "Leo, I—"

"Look, I meant what I said. We're not in a relationship. You're free to see, date, or love anyone you want."

"Love?" I shut my eyes. "No, you don't understand—"

He lifts a palm. "I don't need to know. I'm your boss. You're my employee. What you do on your time is your business. We are platonic. Professional. Though it seems a little fast," he fumes under his breath, and oh, my God. He's jealous.

"Leo, seriously. You have nothing to be jealous about."

"I'm not jealous," he scoffs.

"You're the one spouting off how platonic and professional we are."

"Don't remind me," he seethes. "Here."

He holds up a small white card with six digits on it. "What's this?" I ask as I take it.

"The code. It unlocks the front door."

"I figured you'd have some crazy technology like facial recognition or palm print scanners. Maybe a robot that greets me with a drink."

His eyes narrow, unamused. "Probationary period. Remember?"

His words are hollow. Whatever closeness we've shared is gone. "Of course."

Having just handed me the keys to this kingdom, Leo walks away. And I can't help wishing I could have this family and Leo, too.

I watch as Trini walks further around the lake, letting little Fluff keep up with her. It's as if she's taught the little swan to heel.

"How did it go?" Smoke asks as I approach.

"Not bad. I might have signed away the rights to my first born, but it's done." Trini is far enough out of earshot that I can seize the small opportunity to speak with Smoke. "Thank you."

"For what?" he says, selecting a few small stones from the lakefront.

"For hiring me."

He's careful in selecting a rock from his hand, then flicks it across the lake. It skips along the water six times before vanishing below the surface. "I didn't," he says. "The position is Leo's to do with as he will. Whether or not you were hired was completely his call." He hands me a smooth, flat rock, demonstrating how I could hold it.

I mimic his grasp, aiming at some imaginary target far in the center of the lake. "I was under the impression he didn't want me around." I flick it. It skips four times before sinking below the water.

Smoke drops the remaining rocks to the ground and dusts his hands on his pants. There's a trace of a smile that manages to meet his eyes. "I think you and I both know that isn't what he wants."

CHAPTER 21

Leo

ove you, too. Mindlessly, I click through several more screens. *Unbelievable.*

Was she lying when she said she didn't have a boyfriend? Or is she back with that numbnuts at the assisted living facility? "Derrick," I say, disgusted. From what I've been able to piece together, the entire time he and Ivy dated, he's been with no less than three other women and is about to drive his personal finances into bankruptcy. "What the fuck does she see in this guy?"

Knock-knock-knock.

I check the clock. Midnight. The light tapping at the door has me to my feet in an instant. *Trinity?*

I throw on my sweats but forgo the shirt when the knocks grow louder. As soon as I crack open the door, I regret it.

"Can we talk?" Ivy asks. I immediately notice she's in a flannel pajama top and boy shorts with her hair dripping wet from the shower. Coming here wasn't planned. Something's wrong.

"What is it? Is it Trinity?"

"No, I just . . . " She bites her lower lip. "I think we should talk."

This is a bad idea. An idiotically bad idea. But the second she says *please*, my brain misfires. I open the door wider. "Come in."

Slowly, she makes her way into the room. Much like Trinity did, she takes in every photograph and book. Her fingers brush the pillow with Noble's image stitched across it. "It's beautiful," she says.

"Trini made it."

Her nod is slight and sad. She notices my laptop. Images from her past. A chronology of her life. All of it at my fingertips. I watch as she takes a good long look before turning those big brown eyes to me.

We stare at each other for a long moment. "What do you want?" I ask, breaking the silence.

Her words stammer. "I wanted to . . . to thank you. For hiring me. I know you didn't want to," she says, twisting her lips with a sad smile. "Why did you do it?"

Why? Because I'm an idiot who thinks I can have my cake and eat it, too. Because I haven't learned my lesson—when I'm distracted, bad things happen to people I care about.

Because I care about you. Because I want more. Because I want. You.

Instead of saying any of that, I step into her space. "It doesn't matter. You should go."

Her nod is slight as she returns the pillow where she got it and heads toward the door, stopping just shy of it. "I wasn't talking to a guy earlier," she explains, turning to face me. "When I said, 'Love you, too,' I was talking to my aunt."

"Your aunt?" I ask, realizing I've caught Ivy in a lie so sloppy, it's pathetic. I close in on her.

"Mm-hmm," she says, taking two steps back as I move even closer, caging her against the wall. "What are you doing, Leo?" she asks, a question in her eyes.

I keep my rage to a low simmer, wrapping a gentle hand

around her neck. The wild thump of her pulse grows. I huff. "I'm disappointed, Ivy. I thought you'd be better at this."

She shakes her head. "Better at what?"

"Lying," I seethe. Her eyes widen, fear behind them. Clearly, she has no idea who I am or what I do. "I know everything about you."

"You do?"

Mentally, I flip through the facts. Mother: Samara Palmer. An only child. Drunk and strung out, and once actually tried to sell Ivy for a fix. A fact that makes me sick to my stomach and one that the sheriff's office tried to hide, but I found it. Along with a dozen other horrifying things no child should endure.

And where was her father in all this? As far as I can tell, the man is a ghost. Non-existent to the point that on Ivy's birth certificate, the space where her father's name should be was deliberately blank. She has no family. And she sure as hell has no aunt.

I should do it. Slice her with every unpleasant part of her past. I can deal with almost anything. But lies? Lies have consequences. I am the consequence. It would be so easy to do it. Hurt her. Scare her. Chase her far away from here. Away from me.

Why have I stopped?

Her palms are warm against my chest, up my neck. On my jaw. "Leo?"

Rage fires through me. I yank her wrists over her head, hard against the wall. "Stop lying. You come here dripping wet from the shower. At midnight. To tell me *thank you*? That the conversation I heard with my own ears was with some aunt?"

"It was," she whispers as her chest raises and lowers faster. Her feeble attempt to wriggle away fades as she gives up. "Do it," she says. Her small body begins to tremble despite her defiance.

My interest is piqued. She can't begin to imagine what I have in store when she lies. "Do what?" I tighten my grip around her wrists. She winces, the small whimper giving me a taste of her fear. Her pain. Impatient, I snap. "Do what?"

A tear fights free. "Hurt me. Punish me for staying. That's what you want, isn't it?"

I nod. "And for lying."

"I haven't lied. I came here to tell you—"

"I already know."

Surprise fills her expression. "You do?"

I nod. "You don't have an aunt."

"What?" Her face twists. "Yes, I do," she pleads, trying to reason with me.

"I don't believe you." I release her, disgusted. I open the door. "Go."

Stupid and stubborn, she shuts it. "No. I'm not leaving. Not until you believe me so we can discuss—"

"Fine," I cut her off, over with this conversation. She has no idea how easy it is for me to shut off my soul. "Turn around."

"Why?"

"You want me to believe you? Then let me show you how I uncover the truth. It's not too late to leave."

She doesn't run like she should. She does what she's told. She turns around, hugging the wall. My hand lands on her ass, angry and hard. "Who were you on the phone with?"

"My aunt," she insists so innocently, it must be practiced.

I grip her hair, fisting her damp ink-black waves until she yelps. "I'm just getting started. The door's right there." I don't wait for her answer before laying down another hard smack.

Again, she takes it.

The more my fury builds, the calmer my tone. "Stop lying about an aunt. Tell me who he is." Adrenaline pumps hard through my veins as I accept my role. All I need is a name. One name. Whoever he is, I'll punish him, too. My hand cracks her ass so hard, it throws her into the wall.

Sobs starts. I expect her to confess. To beg me to stop. To break.

Instead, she stays with her story. "Leo, please. She is my aunt."

Unfeeling, I lean to her ear. It's there. That scent. Her. And I shut it down. "Your lies have earned this, Ivy. Remember that."

If she didn't know who I was before, she will soon enough.

This time I consider the strike. It's one I know will hurt—leave a bruise. It's what she deserves as she spews more lies.

"She's mine as much as I'm hers," Ivy cries, and I drown her out. "As much as she's Brooke's. I love her. And she loves me." She sobs. She's strong. Stubborn.

I'm ready with a punishing blow when I freeze. An image comes to me. Red hair. Green eyes. Her friend, Brooke. Everly. Sheriff Everly's daughter. The same sheriff that tried to seal her mother's records. The one with the sister—Grace.

Grace Everly. *Aunt Grace.*

I stare at my arm, mid-swing. *What am I doing? What have I done?*

Stunned, I release my grip and strain to lower my hand. In a detached state, I stare. Slowly, Ivy turns in place. Harmed because of me. Crying because of me.

Red and weepy, her eyes search mine. In warning, I growl. "You have to leave. Now."

Softly, her hands stroke my jaw. The gentleness is undeserved.

"Do you believe me?" she asks, her breath shaky.

I'm empty. Devoid of any connection. "What does it matter?"

"Because I need you to believe me, no matter what I tell you." More tears stream down her cheeks. "I need you, Leo. Need this. Do you believe me?"

I nod, swiping the wetness from her cheek. Frowning, my forehead falls into hers. "Do you understand now? Why you should keep your distance? Why you should go?"

She shivers. "I'm not leaving. Not like this." Her kiss meets my lips.

Why hasn't she left? Her kiss was soft and feeling. Mine is rough and fevered. Controlling. Possessive. When she whimpers, I grapple for control. "I won't be gentle. I can't."

"Then show me who you are, Leo," she whispers to my mouth.

Her fingers trail lightly down my abs until her nails slice beneath the hem of my sweats. And I know. She doesn't want gentle or sweet. She wants me just like this. Tortured. Pained. Angry at everything that's gone wrong in my life, and angrier still that she's here in Chicago . . . in a dangerous space where, despite my confidence and arrogance, only time will tell if I have the fortitude to do what I need to do. Protect the D'Angelos while keeping her safe.

My training says to send her away, but my instincts are stronger. Feral.

I peel away her clothes and slide a finger between her legs. She parts them. I've barely touched her, and she shivers, soaked and moving her body in an eager rhythm against my hand.

"Is this what you want?" I ask low.

Ivy's voice comes out on a ragged plea. "Please."

The more she chases her desperate need against my fingers, the longer I tease her orgasm, dangling its promise just out of reach until I whip my hand from her thighs. Her whimper drives a wedge between my sanity and self-control.

I line up the head of my cock at her hot entrance, a move that makes me sure I'm seconds from ramming the gates of both heaven and hell—like Ivy holds the keys to my damnation and my salvation all at once.

Uncontrolled, I push inside with one forceful thrust, driving all my anger and pain into her in the worst possible way, showing her that I'm a monster. One she needs to walk away from.

Her cry is soft, but it's enough to wake the madman from his trance.

Ivy.

I need this. Her. The tight grip I have on her hips unlocks, but before I pull out completely, she runs her hands up my thighs, and this time, she's the one taking me.

It's her turn to thrust. To take this lust between us to blazing fire so carnal and raw that nothing exists but the feel of her heat and the scent of her body and my desperate need for her.

I can't think or speak or stop. In the space of her thrusts and mine, I simply am. And as soon as the rush of her climax explodes, I come with such force, it takes all my strength to keep from crushing her against the wall.

All I can do is hold her up. Hold her close. Hold her tight.

Because the thought of letting her go finishes me.

CHAPTER 22
Leo

My hand rests on the hip of the sleeping goddess beside me. In my bed. A bed no other woman has slept in. Or ever will.

She stirs, and I dread that our time is being stolen by the morning ahead. Why can't I have this? Her?

A month ago, Trini's healing was microscopic. Undetectable to the naked eye. The only change is Ivy, breathing new life into everything she touches. Even me.

"What time is it?" she whispers.

"Early. Too early." My lips brush her shoulder. "Sleep. Before I fuck you back to sleep."

Her giggle is groggy as her body moves to escape. "I should go. Before anyone sees."

I hold my tongue. I can't break it to her that half a dozen people already know. My security teams are held to their diligence as much as their discretion. And saying anything now would lead to questions and concerns, and the less incentive she has to leave at this moment, the better.

Kiss after kiss, I make my way between her breasts, down her soft stomach, and between her legs. "That's it. You're getting it."

139

Her legs widen, ready to receive me. "I've been looking for a cure to my insomnia."

I slice a lick across her, and her back arches in response. "You've found it."

By the time I wake, the bed is cold, and her addictive body is gone. At nearly five in the morning, I shower before heading into my day. The laptop with Ivy's life splashed across the screen has died, and I'm in no hurry to revive it.

I want Ivy in my life. Personal. Professional. I'm blurring those lines like a Bob Ross painting, and my fuck-o-meter could give two shits less. I haven't wanted for anything in a very long time, and I want this. The one-night stand I was so determined to lose.

I want Ivy.

Without any official meetings today, I can take on the world in dressed down jeans and a T-shirt, with a jacket that hides the fact I'm wearing my Glock. Not because I have any issues with it but because I don't want it bothering Trini. Or Ivy.

The quiet in the house should be normal for the hour of the day, but something's off. Even from the far end of the hall, I can see the men who should be on point are inexplicably missing.

I check my cell. No alarms. No texts.

I bypass the coffee and follow my gut, making my way to the first-floor security center. As soon as I enter, chaos. Half the team is checking screens while the other half is barking orders to the men on the grounds.

"What the fuck is going on?"

Hunter, freshly tanned and back from Hawaii, has resumed lead and answers for the team. "Trinity is missing."

"What?" I hold up my phone. "There's nothing on my phone and nobody came to my room, so that's impossible, right?"

Guilty looks cross all the men's faces, but no one says a word. I lose it. "Talk!"

"No one wanted to disturb you, sir," Hunter spits out before a decided glance away. I wouldn't exactly call this merciless killer demure, so his sudden shyness pisses me off. I know what he's thinking. What they're all thinking.

Furious, tightness consumes my neck and jaw. Clinging to my composure, I pocket my hands. "I'm not sure at what point my love life became more important than protecting the D'Angelos, but that shit stops now." My heated glare travels from face to face. "Before I kill each of you with my bare hands, how long have you been looking?"

"Thirty minutes."

"And you're still looking. Which means you don't have eyes on her, but you've isolated her last known whereabouts, correct?"

"Yes, sir," bark back several men.

"Where's her phone?"

"We found it in the garden."

"What happened?"

Hunter responds. "Forty-five minutes ago, she left the house."

"Sleepwalking?" I ask, noting the time.

He shakes his head. "Her movements were too deliberate. We had eyes on her until she disappeared into the tree line. We've been searching for her since."

My attention isn't on the two dozen monitors casing the house or grounds. It's on the weather. Rain. The faint drizzle that began around midnight now storms down in cold, dark sheets. *Fuck.*

Monitor six shows a full garage. All cars accounted for. Trini is cold and wet and on foot. "Where are you?" I mutter senselessly under my breath.

Two monitors below, I lock on to the silhouette in the second-floor hall. Ivy. Fully dressed, she knocks twice on Trini's door before cautiously entering. With this elite team of ex-Special Ops, there's no way Trini has returned.

"Where was she last seen? Show me." They point to the forest at the north end of the property. "You have exactly half an hour to have eyes on her. Has anyone checked her room?"

Blank stares.

"I'll do it. Have an ATV ready for my return." Their *Yes, Sirs* are drowned out by the thumping pulse in my ears. I march through the hall, take the stairs two at a time, and plow down Trini's door. Startled, Ivy jumps.

"Why are you here?" I snap, demanding an instant response.

Stammering, she answers. "I just checked my phone. Trini asked for me."

"When?" Her tender eyes search mine. Whatever closeness she needs, I shut down. "When?" I bark.

Her eyes slam shut. "Two hours ago." The moment Ivy tried to leave my bed. That was my second mistake. Stopping her from leaving. My first mistake was keeping her there, to begin with.

I have one job to do. And I blew it.

"Two hours ago?" Smoke shouts, barging in, panic across his expression. "Why are you just now getting here? This is going to be your job, Ivy. You can't sleep through—"

I step between them, ready to face off against my own bad judgment. "She was with me."

"Leo." Ivy's voice is slight as her arms land on my shoulders.

I shrug her off with a sharp question. "What did her text say? *Exactly* what did it say?"

Ivy reads her phone, and it pisses me off that she has to check. How can she not just know this?

"She asked if I could drop by." Ivy shakes her head. "She added these numbers. Today's date."

Smoke and I exchange a pained glance. The anniversary of her attack. I raise two hands in surrender as much as reassurance. "We'll find her, Smoke. *I'll* find her."

The angst in Smoke's eyes scores my heart. "Then do it," he says.

I'm at the waiting ATV in under a minute. Ivy climbs in beside me. "Get out."

"She needs me, too."

"We don't have time for this," I shout.

"Then drive," she cries back, hysterical.

Boiling over, I slam the gas, racing aimlessly to the tree line.

"What does the date mean?" Ivy hollers over the rain.

My jaw clenches tight. I say nothing.

She begs. "I can help, Leo. I know I can help, but I need to know what it means."

Frustrated, I'm on instinct and cut a hard left, nearly throwing her from the velocity. Ivy is not a help. She's a distraction.

"Leo, please."

"It's the anniversary of her attack," I scream, fighting to see through the downpour of rain. My vision blurs with outrage and regret.

"There," Ivy shouts, pointing to a dense thicket of trees.

I drive blind, following her direction despite Trini's last known position. Whatever Ivy sees, I don't. But we're surrounded by trees in no time.

"Trini," she hollers, jumping out of the moving vehicle before I've completely stopped. Her hands cup her mouth, lifting her volume despite the deafening rain. "Trinity!" she shouts, racing in circles.

I scan the trees, desperate to make sense of why we stopped. It's familiar. Why is it familiar?

A faint voice barely registers. "Here."

I look up, shielding my eyes from the pellets of rain. Trini waves from the makeshift window of the treehouse. Ivy is already halfway up, while I'm nearly on my knees with relief.

I try the first rung of the old rope. It breaks. "Shit." Ivy was a pixie, flying up the rope with ease. I, on the other hand, am a giant, half-a-step from sliding down a beanstalk. The old wet rope can't take my weight.

I latch on to a sturdy branch and climb. Branch after slick branch, I struggle to make it to the top. The treehouse is nearly three stories up. What the hell? Did the D'Angelos hire an architect?

Out of breath, I reach the landing. Trini and Ivy hoist me up. The two are all muscles as they plant my body center stage. Definitely stronger than they look.

Winded, I take a long glance down. What if Trini had fallen? A fall from this height is guaranteed to break any number of bones, including her neck.

Beside me, Trini looks down as well before giving me those big, apologetic eyes and a nervous smile. I'm one rational thought from shaking some sense into her. Instead, I take a breath and play it cool, slicking a hand through my wet hair. "What's going on?" I ask as if we're bumping into each other at Starbucks.

She shrugs. "I needed to get out of the rain."

I try not to glare, but that makes absolutely no fucking sense. At all. "Was the house too warm and dry?"

"I needed to clear my head," she says as if that explains everything away.

I call Smoke while texting the team to stand down. "Found her. Hide and seek ends at your old treehouse."

"On my way," he says.

"I'm fine," Trini announces to the phone.

"Bring a blanket." Considering Smoke is an even bigger ogre than I am, I slip in, "And a ladder."

His long huff is audible before he disconnects. Mine is quieter. More meditative. Ivy's words are gentle as she rubs Trini's arms, and Trini tries to hide a shiver. I undo my jacket. "We were worried," Ivy says.

My jacket is around Trinity before she can object. She fishes her arms into it. "I . . . couldn't sleep." She turns to Ivy, softening her voice. "I texted you. But it was late."

"She'll never miss a text from you again," I reply for Ivy. My tone is harsh. It has to be. Ivy was as distracted by me as I was by her. This is my wake-up call. Trinity is safe this time, but what about the next?

I have one job to do, and that job isn't Ivy. There will be no next time.

I keep constant watch for the Range Rover, ready with the flashlight on my phone to signal him. Trini and Ivy huddle together, splitting my coat so each has an arm in each sleeve. It's ridiculous. And adorable. And I can't break up whatever the hell this is between them.

"I remember . . . something," Trini confides as she struggles with her words. Ivy listens and caresses her hand as I latch on to every word. A memory, any memory, is all we need.

"It's okay," Ivy reassures her. "Take your time."

"It happened at night. I remember, but everything else is foggy. Disjointed. I thought if I went outside, walked around, I'd remember more. When the rain turned torrential, I lost my bearings. It wasn't until I found the treehouse that I knew where I was. I figured I'd wait here until the rain let up." Regretful, she looks up at me. "I'm sorry."

Before I say a word, Ivy grabs the old plastic phone off the wall and proceeds to scold her. "The least you could've done is called." The worried crease in Trini's forehead vanishes as the two giggle lightly. Ivy's good for Trinity. Too bad she's pure kryptonite for me.

"How did you know I was here?" Trinity asks Ivy, and my ears perk up. She's either fucking psychic or this woman knows more about Trinity and Smoke than she's let on.

"The photo on Smoke's desk. The treehouse is in the background. It was a longshot, but when I saw it in the distance—"

The loud engine of Smoke's SUV blazing through has both girls on their feet. I signal him in though I'm not sure how necessary it is. He and two men jump out, and a long ladder is secured in place. "D'Angelo Rescue, at your service."

When we return to the house, I avoid Ivy. And my men have strict instructions to keep her far away from me.

I have enough work to keep me occupied for days. Whatever analysis I was doing on Olivia Ann Palmer can wait. All reasons to pry further into her life are ceased. Shoved to a backburner I don't intend on revisiting it anytime soon.

It's my only way out of making more mistakes. Ivy is the sun. And I am Icarus. Foolish enough to believe that one touch won't cost me everything.

CHAPTER 23

Ivy

"Let me help you," I say to Trinity, wanting to learn more about the amazing meals she likes to prepare on Sundays.

Smoke told me this is new, only since I started working here. I wonder if it's something Trinity has always wanted to do, share her love of cooking with someone who's equally as interested in rustic Italian cuisine.

And I do want to learn. This is my heritage, and I'm grateful that Trinity is here to hand it to me. I want to do everything I can to embrace our family traditions. Anything at all to keep my mind engaged and focused so I don't obsess about the man I've barely spoken to since he destroyed me three weeks ago.

Twenty days. That's how long he and Smoke and six members of the security team have been gone. Smoke calls Trinity twice a day. But I haven't heard from Leo. Not a text or a call. Not a word. I need to tell him. Who I am. Why I'm here. But Leo is unreachable, physically and emotionally. There's nothing I can do but wait him out because I can't exactly confess to a ghost.

Trinity scoops another pile of flour in front of me, and I mimic what she does to hers. "Make a well so the mound of flour resembles a volcano," she says, and I do, thinking how this is like science class. "Now add the eggs."

I crack the eggs one by one. Watching them fall feels like therapy. Snippets of time when I forget about Leo and focus on something—anything—else. Working the dough, I pour myself into breaking it down to build it back up into something beautiful and new. Like a phoenix rising out of the dough to form spaghetti or ravioli or lasagna.

I've grown to love Sundays, the time when Trinity shares all her family stories with me. She paints a picture of always having her parents and brothers around. When life was good times and laughter, and family was everything. She has five brothers in total, and in all this time, I've only met Smoke. What keeps them away?

Even with a house full of people—it's easy to feel the chill of isolation and loneliness. With round-the-clock security teams hovering about, they're here to work. Trinity would be all alone if she weren't with me. And I find myself in the same boat.

Smoke and Leo are returning today—a fact I only know because of Trinity whipping up a special feast for their return. She's gone all out, preparing burrata and cherry tomatoes with olive oil and fresh basil for an appetizer and cannoli for dessert. I have no idea how I lived before trying my first cannoli.

While Trinity gets dressed for dinner, I'm cleaning up the kitchen alone.

"Hey."

Startled, I whirl around at the familiar voice.

Leo's scruff is a little longer than it was when I saw him last, and I tamp down the small worry that surfaces. In a dark gray button-down and with his wavy hair damp from a recent shower, he hasn't shaved as he normally would. It could be a new look for him, but it feels like something more. Like his coming home will be fleeting, and I can't help but wonder if he'll even stay the night.

I've tried not wanting Leo—not letting hope bloom when I see him—but it's not easy. Settling for professional and platonic feels unobtainable. Leo is oxygen. I've never needed someone more.

"Hey, yourself," I say, snapping the flour container shut so I can put it away.

Hey is the most Leo has said to me since our explosive night together, though technically, I report to him. The day I accepted the job, I wasn't sure he'd ever speak to me again. It's weird to miss someone when the only promise shared between us was simple. No commitments.

When I try to reach the high shelf this special Italian flour is usually kept on, Leo steps in. "Let me."

He moves too close to me, and once he has the flour back in its original place, we both pause, the air between us electric and charged. He reaches out and brushes what I'm sure is flour from my cheek before a flash of regret crosses his features.

Pocketing his hands, he takes a deliberate step away. "Something smells good." Prowling to the stove, he lifts lids to get a better look at the feast awaiting us all.

"I'm glad you and Smoke are back. Safe and sound."

It's the world I've come to know better, even if I don't completely understand it. When they leave, nothing is discussed. At least, not openly.

Smoke and Leo and a few members of the security team take off in the middle of the night with enough weapons for a small military strike team. The only way I even know Leo will be gone by morning is that look in his eyes. An arctic chill sweeps over them, and the normally bright blue hardens to an empty darkness I don't recognize and can't seem to reach.

That's when I lose Leo to Z, a man my heart bleeds so much harder for.

For no reason at all, I tiptoe close until we're a breath apart. My lips reach his, wrapping my arms around his neck until this kiss tells him everything I haven't. Everything I can't. Who I am. Why

I'm here. And how much I need him to be okay with it all, because I need him.

Leo's kiss is pained, and the strong arms that would usually sweep me against his body don't. "You mean a lot to me, Ivy. You care so much about everyone. Especially Trinity."

You mean a lot to me, too.

I think the words but don't say them, afraid to disturb our intimacy. Instead, I simply stand there, studying his eyes. I don't see the cold mercenary the world knows as Z. But somehow, I don't see the familiar warmth of Leo either.

He lets out a sigh and looks away. "Which is why this is so hard to say."

A lump forms in my throat. *Is he trying to fire me again?*

"Say what, Leo?"

"I can't lead you on, Ivy. And I can't keep using you."

His soft words slice into my heart like an icy blade, and I blink hard, searching his expression. Nothing makes sense.

"Using me? I don't understand."

His hands are loose around my wrists, keeping me distant but forcing me to listen. "There's someone else."

It takes a second before I feel my body again, but when his thumbs wipe fresh tears from my cheeks, I can't stop what comes over me. I explode, pounding into his chest, shoving him away. But I'm no match for his gentle grip on my wrists, and trying to break free is pointless. He's still holding me. Why is he still holding me?

"Let go."

"Not until you hear all of it."

"Hear how in the span of twenty days, you met someone else? Pass." Wiggling to escape does no good.

"I haven't met anyone else," he says, holding me tight until my rage settles enough for him to continue. "It's my wife."

"Wife? You're married?"

I'm floored. And outraged. Furious, I swing at him, but my slap falls short, landing in his grip. Again, he doesn't let go.

"Lori died two years ago, and I was helpless to stop it. In more ways than I can explain, the best parts of me died with her." The mourning in Leo's eyes is raw and deep, and it tears me apart. He sucks in a breath, avoiding my eyes. "I can't give you my heart, Ivy. After our last night together, I realized the truth. You deserve someone who'll always put you first. You deserve better."

His tender kiss on my temple feels strange and final, and my heart beats hard as my mind whirls.

It isn't true. It can't be true.

But what if it is? What if the passion between us was a lightning strike—a white-hot flare in the moment, never to happen again?

Leo releases my wrists and is already halfway across the room before I can react. "You can come in, Hunter."

As the large man enters, I swipe the remaining traces of heartbreak from my cheeks.

Despite my heart landing somewhere on the floor before him, Leo speaks only to Hunter. "Ivy, this is Hunter. You'll now report to him. I'll leave you to introduce yourself. Take care of her."

The two men shake hands like some really fucked up passing of the guard. Without another word, Leo leaves, and I'm left with the burly titan.

True to his namesake, Hunter is slow in his approach as if he knows with any sudden movements, I'll bolt. "It's a pleasure to meet you, Ivy."

He holds out a hand, but I ignore it. My suspicion gets the better of me.

"I've met everyone in this household, and I've never seen you."

He gives me a shy smile, one that looks way too practiced as if he's used it a million times before to get whatever he wants. Access to information or panties, it's all the same to a man like him.

And I'm on to him. Oh, am I on to him.

"Right," he says, rubbing the back of his neck to show off his tanned bicep and the tattoos peeking beneath the tight sleeve of his

T-shirt. "Before the work I just did with Leo, I was at my sister's wedding. In Hawaii. I took a few extra days to explore the islands. Have you ever been?"

I let my scowl answer, though he's being really, really nice. And if Leo meant it, this man is now my boss. Making a good impression would be smart. But I'm suffocating in the loss of Leo's presence and his self-righteous one-way conversation, and all I want to do is fuck some sense into him.

"Excuse me," I say like an idiot because I'm pretty sure Hunter was mid-sentence, giving me some rare tidbit about traveling to the isle of paradise in the middle of the Pacific.

I can't put my finger on it, but something's off. This wasn't just about sex, as beyond mind-blowing as it was. There's something more between us. Leo and I have a connection, and I can't be the only one feeling it.

Leo didn't flinch when he pulled a gun on a lowlife thief or the rich and powerful Uncle Andre. But face to face with me, he couldn't meet my eyes? And Hunter. Freshly tanned and happens to be waiting in the wings? Maybe I'm clinging too hard to a man eager to let me go, but everything feels like a lie.

Pushing past my tears and pain, I race down the long length of hall to his room. When pounding on the door does nothing, I try the knob. It opens.

"Leo?"

I step inside, but the room is empty. Not only is Leo not here, but none of his things are.

The nightstands. The chairs. The desk. Even his oversized king bed is gone—the one I woke up in with nothing covering me but his strong arms and tender kisses. Where less than a month ago, nothing existed but his heartbeat against mine.

Leo is gone. And all evidence that we've been anything at all is suddenly erased.

CHAPTER 24
Leo

"It's done," I say, steeling myself for the work ahead.

Smoke studies me, then nods. "What did you tell her?" he asks.

Despite the need to tell him to fuck off and mind his own business, I keep my response vague. "Something believable. Something I knew would work."

He nods in a solidary show of support before leveling me with his opinion. "Having a life isn't a crime."

"It is when you're me," I reply, reminding him, "I have a job to do."

"Nothing happened," he argues. "Trinity is fine."

"And what about the next time?"

He has no answer, and neither do I. Rather than prolong the argument, Smoke rummages through a box of John Grisham books from my room, pulling out a paperback I don't recognize. "Here," he says, tossing me the flitty book.

I catch it, coming face to face with a shirtless man in a kilt. Glaring, I notice the title. *"Ivy's Passion."*

"Too soon?" he smirks. "I found that in your closet."

Annoyed, I raise a brow. He chuckles. "That room wasn't always yours. It's like the universe is trying to tell you something."

"That my boss is a dickhead? Or that crazy Aunt Sonia was a mad fan of the bagpipe?" I flip through the pages. "Worst house-warming gift ever. The least you could do is get me a hardcover."

"I'm saving that for Christmas." Smoke glances across the room. "Nice digs."

He should know, considering it's his property. I've kept almost everything intact. Everything but the bedroom. Ivy is the only woman who's ever been in that bed, and that bed stays with me. An image of my finger tracing the long line of her thigh is instantly shut down. "The north house is ideal," I reply, offering Smoke a decanter of scotch that's been here for who knows how long. Smartly, he declines.

"Ideally located," he says, glancing out the window. I know what he's looking at. Let him. "It's hidden behind the woods, but I can keep tabs on things. And it's big enough to house your brothers without drawing unnecessary attention. Especially with Andre snooping around."

"And Ivy?" Smoke's question is sharp, a pinprick I quickly recover from.

"Andre's interest in her can't be a coincidence, and orchestrating her arrest took way more planning that he'd ever devote to an outsider. That, along with the theft of her credit card as soon as she arrived in the state, makes me certain she's being targeted. I've got Hunter on her."

Smoke's brows quirk in surprise. "Ivy won't have an issue with a deadly assassin hovering around her like a helicopter parent?"

"As far as she knows, he's her boss."

I glance out the window through an area of brush and trees I've trimmed back. The light in Ivy's room has just been switched on. Even from this distance, I notice everything from Mr. Whiskers on her pillow to the robe draped across her bed . . . to her.

The private moment Ivy steals to stare out the window and cry consumes me. It claws at the heart I swore I couldn't give her. And there's nothing I can do about it.

If I were any other man, she'd already be mine. And in the cruelest twist of fate, she is. Ivy Palmer will forever be mine to protect. A purgatory I willingly accept as long as it keeps her safe.

I stare longer than I should, wondering if she'll bail on dinner like I will.

I shoot Hunter a quick text.

Me: See if she prefers dinner in her room.
Hunter: Yes, sir.

"When do your brothers arrive?" I ask, refocusing back to the conversation.

"Next week," Smoke says.

"All of them?" I ask to clarify. "A shift in the D'Angelo center of gravity of this magnitude means heightened security. Especially when the lot of you are so fucking volatile, you'll need the most protection from each other. Thank God I'm focused on my work."

"Thank God." Smoke's pat on the shoulder is brotherly, sympathetic as he heads out the door.

As soon as he's gone, I gravitate back to the window.

When Hunter arrives with her food, I notice the boyish grin as much as the single long-stemmed rose in a vase. For fuck's sake, what is he? The Bachelor? I'm busy selecting his headstone when she saves his life and sends him away.

There's a part of me that doesn't blame him, even if I do end up killing him. Ivy is kind and generous. Brave and strong. Addictive. Breathtaking. I can't give her my heart because she already has it. Whether she knows it or not.

I'm not ready to let her go. I'll never be ready.

When she sets aside the food and collapses on the bed, not going to her—not holding her—tortures me.

But this is the life I've chosen. The one where everyone I care for is safe.

With one final glance, I shut the drapes and wall off my heart. "Goodbye, Ivy."

Thank you for reading SINS of the Syndicate! I hope you love Leo and Ivy as much as I do. The next book in the SINS series continues their love story. ORDER BOOK 2 NOW!

Leo
I'll never stop protecting her.
Watching her.
Wanting her.

SINS of the Syndicate >> CLICK FOR BOOK 2!

How about something a little Ruthless?

Power plays are hard.

Trying to one up the stranger who banged me senseless last night?

Definitely harder.

Available on All Platforms! **Get RUTHLESS WARS Now>**

. . .

"Tons of chemistry and passion ... Highly addictive" ~*Goodreads Reviewer*

Join Lexxi's VIP reader list to be the first to know of new releases, free books, special prices, and other giveaways!

Free hot romances & happily ever afters delivered to your inbox.
https://www.lexxijames.com/freebies

About the Author

Lexxi James is a best-selling author of romantic suspense. Her feats in multi-tasking include binge watching Netflix and sucking down a cappuccino in between feverish typing and loads of laundry.

She lives in Ohio with her teen daughter and the sweetest man in the universe. She loves to hear from readers!

www.LexxiJames.com